She couldn't believe how much she wanted Alex...

Everything from his voice to the crinkle of his eyes when he smiled hit Meg where it counted. Yeah, it probably didn't help that she hadn't had sex since the Ice Age.

Time. That's all she needed. Time to feel as if the man sprawled on her bed was the same man she liked so much online.

Meg felt her cheeks fill with heat. She'd told him so much about herself. They hadn't actually had sex, of course. But the man definitely had a starring role in all her sexual fantasies.

Which they'd discussed. In detail.

She knew Alex liked things intense. That he was a very oral kind of guy. And that he had a thing for white panties.

Should she just pounce on him? It wasn't her style. Not that she *had* an actual style, but jumping him after an hour and a half together seemed…excessive. So how long was enough? Four hours? Five?

Of course, she'd known him a year online. *More* than enough time, Meg thought, grinning. She might not jump him in the next ten minutes, but it wouldn't be long.…

Dear Reader,

I don't know about you, but when I daydream about a perfect setting for romance, there's always a beach involved. Soft breezes, warm sand, puffy white clouds and a gorgeous man in a hammock. That's where I lived while writing Meg and Alex's story for 24 HOURS: ISLAND FLING. Okay, so it was all in my imagination but surely that counts.

I got the idea for *Minute by Minute* because so many of my girlfriends have been meeting men online. The conversations have been intimate, revealing, enticing and very, very safe until they decide to meet in person. That's when things get... interesting.

Was he telling the truth? Will he be as funny? As kind? As sexy? Will it be as easy to talk when you're lying together in that hammock? There are so many things that can go right or wrong and it all comes down to the first 24 hours! So get ready for a wild ride, and don't forget your piña colada!

I hope you enjoy all the books in the 24 HOURS: ISLAND FLING miniseries. And don't forget to check out my Web site at www.joleigh.com.

Cheers,

Jo Leigh

Books by Jo Leigh

HARLEQUIN BLAZE

*Do Not Disturb

MINUTE BY MINUTE
Jo Leigh

HARLEQUIN®

TORONTO • NEW YORK • LONDON
AMSTERDAM • PARIS • SYDNEY • HAMBURG
STOCKHOLM • ATHENS • TOKYO • MILAN • MADRID
PRAGUE • WARSAW • BUDAPEST • AUCKLAND

To Cara and Kimberly,
for many hours of Island fun!

ISBN 0-373-79231-X

MINUTE BY MINUTE

www.eHarlequin.com

Prologue

[DCWatcher] First…don't be mad, Meg.

[MtnVet] Don't be mad?

[DCWatcher] Yeah.

[MtnVet] About?

[DCWatcher] You need to go to the door.

[MtnVet] My door?

[DCWatcher] Ha, yes. Your front door. I'll wait.

[MtnVet] Be right back.

[MtnVet] Alex, what is this?

[DCWatcher] Tell me what you got.

[MtnVet] Flowers. Beautiful, I might add. And a pretty big envelope.

[DCWatcher] I'm glad you like the flowers.

[MtnVet] Calla lilies are my favorites. You knew that, didn't you?

[DCWatcher] I try to pay attention, Meg. Now, open the envelope.

[MtnVet] Alex????

[DCWatcher] It's the island, Meg. I couldn't believe it when I found it. It's everything we talked about. The thatched bungalows, the scuba diving, the hammock in the palm trees.

[MtnVet] We were drunk. It was New Year's Eve.

[DCWatcher] I know. I was there.

[MtnVet] It was a fantasy, Alex.

[DCWatcher] But it doesn't have to be. What's it been, a year now that we've been meeting online like this?

[MtnVet] About that, yeah.

[DCWatcher] So, here's the deal. It's your birthday today. You got me that incredible Mingus album on mine, and I wanted to do something special for you.

So when I found out about Escapades, I said what the hell.

[MtnVet] Alex, there's an airline ticket in here. And a reservation.

[DCWatcher] Five days, four nights. And don't worry. The bungalow has a loft with an extra bed and bathroom. I don't want you feeling any pressure.

[DCWatcher] Meg, you still there?

[MtnVet] I am, but I don't know what to say. We don't even know each other. This is so extravagant.

[DCWatcher] *We don't know each other?* What are you, nuts? I've told you more about myself than any other living human. And honey, the things I know about you...

[MtnVet] Yeah, yeah. I guess so. I have been incredibly indiscreet, haven't I?

[DCWatcher] Don't worry. I'll never tell a living soul about your spanking fetish.

[MtnVet] Alex!!!

[DCWatcher] Just kidding.

[MtnVet] Jeez, tell a man one little fantasy.

[DCWatcher] Say yes, Meg. I know you need this break. You haven't taken any time off for so long. I don't know how you're walking around, considering all you do.

[MtnVet] I know, but so soon? In two weeks? Oh, man, Valentine's Day?

[DCWatcher] Don't read anything into it. It's when I could get the reservation.

[MtnVet] My ass. But it's sweet anyway. Only, who's going to fill in when I'm gone?

[DCWatcher] How about Scott?

[MtnVet] He didn't get much out of his last stay here.

[DCWatcher] But maybe, if you're gone, your loving patients and their owners will have to turn to him.

[MtnVet] I suppose.

[DCWatcher] Meg, you're stalling. Listen to me. We both need this. I'm tired of just looking at that picture of you, although God knows, you look great. I want to see you. I want to hear your voice, listen to your laugh. It doesn't have to go anywhere. Hell, it can't. I'm in D.C., you're in L.A. But for just five days and four nights, can't the twain meet?

[MtnVet] The twain, huh? I've never heard it put quite like that before.

[DCWatcher] Man, do you have a dirty mind.

[MtnVet] Me? You're one to talk.

[MtnVet] Would you really sleep in the loft?

[DCWatcher] If necessary.

[MtnVet] And this bungalow. It doesn't have a TV?

[DCWatcher] Nope. But it does have room service. And a masseuse.

[MtnVet] Oh, God. That sounds like heaven.

[DCWatcher] So what are you waiting for?

[MtnVet] Alex, what if we hate each other on sight?

[DCWatcher] How could I hate you? You're what I look forward to most every day. I leave the damn computer on all the time, just listening for that little tone announcing I've got mail. Don't you get that by now?

[MtnVet] I'm grinning like an idiot here.

[DCWatcher] That's a good start.

[MtnVet] And that picture of you in the *Washington Post*? You did say it was a recent one, yes?

[DCWatcher] Yep. If you weren't sickened by that, we should be okay in person.

[MtnVet] Well...

[DCWatcher] Come on, woman. Take a risk. What's the worst that could happen?

[DCWatcher] Meg?

[MtnVet] Wait, I'm imagining the worst. It's pretty horrible.

[DCWatcher] Tropical island. Warm breezes. Pure white sand on a private beach. Drinks with tiny umbrellas in them.

[MtnVet] Stop. I can't stand it. Okay. Yes. I'll go.

[DCWatcher] It was the umbrellas, wasn't it?

[MtnVet] You do know me too well.

[DCWatcher] So for real? Yes?

[MtnVet] Yes. Wow.

[DCWatcher] Wow, indeed.

1

IT WAS NOON ON THE dot when the plane, a little propeller job that had flown so close to the ocean Meg could have jumped without a parachute, landed on the island. The view, of rocky cliffs, crystal clear blue waters, and vegetation so green it almost hurt, had stolen her breath, and she wondered if she'd ever get it back.

It didn't help that she was scared spitless. Not about the plane; she loved puddle jumpers. *He* was, theoretically, already here. Since her birthday, she'd hardly been able to think of anything else. She was going to meet Alex Rosten in the flesh. After an entire year of talking to him online in private chats, they were going to be face-to-face in, like, thirty seconds.

Meg waited until everyone else had cleared the aisle, and then she got her travel bag from the overhead compartment. Her body fairly quivered with tension. Although she was trying to be very Zen about the whole experience, she was failing miserably. She wanted to like him. She wanted to be attracted to him. She wanted him to sweep her off her feet.

Problem was, she also wanted not to like him so much, to find him more a friend than a lover, and she needed to keep her feet firmly on the ground.

For a woman whose biggest single risk up to this point was going to UC Davis instead of UCLA, this little vacation was monumental.

Her whole life had been swallowed by her work. Since her father had died and left her his veterinary clinic in Diamond Canyon, she'd been working six days a week. But because she was always on call, time off was more a concept than a reality. Her only personal time was when she was online with Alex.

If they blew this, if the chemistry wasn't there, then what? What would she do on those nights when by some mysterious grace he was there when she was there, and they talked until they both got stupid with tiredness? Until they laughed at the most ridiculous things ever?

She needed Alex. Needed to find him on the other end of the computer, needed the *possibility* that she'd find him. She'd been so fiercely protective of their relationship that they'd never even spoken on the phone. He'd asked, she'd debated, but in the end it seemed safer just to keep the status quo. Which this little trip shattered all to hell.

"May I help you, Miss?"

She turned to the steward, sharp in his khakis, thick eyebrows raised. "No, thanks. I've got it."

She pulled up the handle on her case and rolled it toward the door. Would Alex be on the tarmac or inside? Would she know him immediately, and he know her? And, oh, God, was she supposed to kiss him? Hug? Shake hands?

Pushing her hair back behind her shoulders, she straightened, took a deep breath and stepped onto the portable steps.

Blinking in the tropical sunlight, she scanned the small group of people standing in front of the terminal. The heat hit her hard, not because it was so different from the cold Los Angeles winter but because her fear and anticipation had chilled her deeply. When she thought of the things she'd told him in the late hours, the fantasies she'd revealed in lurid detail… It was hard to breathe as her gaze went from one face to another.

He wasn't there. The impatient noises behind her sent her forward. It was only eleven steps down, and not that far to enter the terminal, but she had to consciously make her legs move.

Maybe he'd chickened out. It was possible, right? She'd hear her name over the loudspeaker, a message at the desk.

Not likely. He'd sent her an e-mail yesterday with his flight information from Dulles. He'd sounded so excited. Which wasn't fair. Shouldn't he be sweating this, too? He probably figured in five days and four nights, he was bound to get lucky, so why worry? What she didn't understand was why she couldn't see things in exactly the same way.

Going by his picture—well, pictures—he was a nice-looking guy. Although the photo of him from the *Washington Post* was too grainy to see him fully, when she'd Googled him, she'd found others. Him with politicians, him getting awards, him being important. He rarely smiled, but there'd been this one… He was alone, leaning against a brick wall, and he looked happy. She remembered finding that picture and thinking about his smile. Such a good smile. Not to mention his expressive eyes and his dark, thick hair. She already knew the most important things about him—that he had a great sense of humor, and that he was really smart, and kind. She should be filled with anticipation—good anticipation, not this sick dread.

If only she hadn't been quite so open. If only she hadn't told him *all* of her secrets…

HE SHOULD HAVE GONE outside. Alex ran a hand through his hair as he paced underneath the huge circular clock above the terminal doors. The plane had landed, and he knew she was out there, so what was he doing in here?

He was behaving like an idiot, like a teenager. At thirty-three, he'd had his share of blind dates, and he'd never given them a second thought. They'd clicked or they hadn't. No sweat. Of course, he'd never been in a situation like this one.

He liked Meg more than anyone he'd met in a hell of a long time, but it was all online, and that wasn't the truest test. Not by a long shot.

His buddy Craig had met a woman online. Through Match.com. They'd talked for three months. She'd lived in Brussels, and Craig had liked her so much he'd paid for her to move to D.C. It was a disaster.

She'd used him, lied, made up just about everything about herself, except for her name.

If Meg had done the same thing, Alex was screwed in more ways than one. Not just because they'd be in such close proximity for five days, but because, despite his best intentions, he had expectations. Which was always, always a mistake.

Don't hope, you can't get hurt, right? Everyone's got their own agenda, and the smiles and the hand-shakes don't mean shit. He'd been in Washington a long time, and he'd learned not to underestimate the depth of deception in the human heart.

No, he wasn't going to think about D.C. He'd spent all day wondering how the press was reacting to his lat-est column. It was either going to be a scandal worthy of congressional investigation, or a blip on the radar, bur-ied somewhere in the back pages. It was out of his hands.

"This is ridiculous," he said, startling the woman next to him. He gave her a smile, then stepped out to meet Meg. And stopped.

Oh, Christ. She was perfect.

MEG BLINKED. It was him. She gripped the handle of her bag as she stared. He was so much more than she'd pic-tured. Taller. Darker hair. Brighter smile. And his eyes were filled with a pleasure she could hardly comprehend.

"Wow."

"I'll say."

He laughed, and it did things to her insides. Then he took the few steps needed to be close. Close enough to touch. "Nice to meet you, Meg Becker."

She grinned. "Nice to meet you, too."

He looked at her. Really looked. First at her face, his eyes crinkling in the bright sunlight, then slowly down her body. He didn't pause, but he didn't rush.

She'd worn a pale green, sleeveless button-down blouse and beige capris. Comfort was her goal, as the trip from L.A. to Florida had been a long one, and then the hop to the island, of course. She'd left her hair down, and it occurred to her that she should have brushed it. Put on fresh lip gloss. At least checked to make sure her makeup hadn't smeared.

When Alex's gaze rose again, he didn't seem displeased. Not if that incredible smile was any indication.

He had to be at least six feet tall. He was wearing a pair of well-worn jeans and the softest looking shirt. The sleeves were rolled up a couple of turns, showing the dark hair, not too thick, on his arms. It wasn't buttoned all the way up, either, so she could see the suggestion of hair on his chest. It made her want to touch him. Feel if his hair was as soft as the sleek cream shirt. If his chest was as hard as she hoped. Altogether, he was kinda built and surprisingly sexy.

She laughed. She wasn't even sure why, except, oh, God, here she was on a tropical island with a man she was seeing for the very first time and they'd been together two seconds and already she wanted to plaster herself to his chest.

Alex laughed, too. It was a great sound. Deep, rich. Quite yummy. Lord, he had dimples. Not little teeny ones, but long commas next to the smile lines bracketing his mouth.

"There's not a flight out until tomorrow," he said, "so it's too late to turn back now."

"I don't want to turn back."

"Thank God. How about I take you to see the island?"

"Sounds great." She stepped closer to him, expecting him to back up and lead her to her baggage, but he didn't move. His eyes had softened, lost their humor but not their spark, and the smile that had been there since he'd opened the door drifted, leaving him with parted lips and a look that told her that no one was going to be using that loft, after all.

2

CHARLIE HANOVER LOWERED THE *POST* to his lap as he swung his leather chair around. He had a great view of the Washington Monument from his office and when it snowed like this he'd often sit and stare for long stretches, just letting his thoughts go where they may.

So Alex Rosten had officially gone 'round the bend. Charlie smiled, letting the moment have its due. That bastard Rosten had been a thorn in his side since college. Charlie didn't care how many times Rosten denied it, he had been the one to start those rumors of plagiarism when they'd both been up for the Balakian Award. It was no coincidence that Alex had won.

Charlie figured he'd be done with Rosten after that, but no. They'd both been up for jobs at the *Post* at the same time, and, again, no coincidence, Alex had triumphed. But now that Charlie was covering Washington for the *New York Times*, Alex could kiss his ass. Although he didn't have to now. With this column, Alex wouldn't have a source left in Washington, or anywhere else for that matter, who'd give him the time of day.

Picking up the paper, he read the article again. He'd give Alex credit—he focused on his own errors of omission. He'd spilled the beans about Senator Allen's birthday bash in Hawaii two years ago. The celebration had been an obscene display of wealth, with everything from barely dressed dancing girls to troughs of the most expensive champagne and caviar in the world. The total price tag had been in excess of two million, most of it taxpayer money. That little detail hadn't hit the papers, even though there had been a large contingent of journalists sipping the bubbly and enjoying the view.

Charlie had been there. Had a great time. He'd gotten a dozen good columns out of that junket, and he had no regrets. You gave a little to get a little. That's the way it worked in Washington. The way it would always work. But Alex, in a fit of ethical remorse, was now sorry he hadn't reported about the misappropriation of funds. He admitted that while he'd suspected the money was tainted, he hadn't dug further. Because, like Charlie, he'd gotten a lot of other juicy tidbits at that shindig. More than just the material for a number of political columns, he'd gotten the biggest single commodity on the Hill—information. The one currency that never loses its value.

According to Alex, he was no longer willing to trade information without full and immediate disclosure to the American people. Noble sentiment. But it would never work. It wasn't how the game was played. Power was everything in Washington, and no bleeding heart would ever change that.

Charlie put the article away as his secretary stepped inside his office. "Talk to me."

"Alex Rosten is gone," Stephanie said. "On vacation."

"Not surprising. Where?"

She frowned. "This is gonna cost you. I had to prom-ise I'd go to dinner with that slimy creep at the *Post*."

"Two three-day weekends?"

"Deal."

"So?"

"He's gone to an island in the Caribbean. To a resort called Escapades. And before you ask, I called around. There are no rooms at the inn."

"Escapades, huh? Don't worry about it. I know a guy. Get me everything we have on Rosten. I want to be out of here in two hours."

"Yes, sir."

Charlie turned to his computer, to his database. He didn't know the owner of Escapades, but he had a buddy who did. And that buddy owed him, big time. Which is how the game was played. Only this time, Charlie was going to make sure Alex Rosten went down in flames.

ALEX HAD ONLY BEEN on the island a few hours, but that didn't stop him from giving Meg a detailed tour. They were in a glorified golf cart, her luggage safely stowed in the back. The island was actually a pretty big place. On one side, the side with the airport, was a full-out lux-ury resort. They passed a large white hotel, curved and glittering and elegant. Near the hotel were several res-taurants, a couple of pools, a spa, tennis courts and more. Everything a person could want, if a person wanted to be around people.

On the other side of the island, where he was taking her, were bungalows. Only twelve, all of them perched either in the seaside palm trees or right over the water. The one he'd booked was over the water. No restaurants, no pools. Just the bluest ocean on earth meeting the bluest skies in the heavens.

They had the use of the cart for the duration of their stay, which meant they could go wherever they chose easily, but he had high hopes that they wouldn't be spending a lot of time at group activities.

"This is breathtaking," Meg said, as they drove by one of the huge swimming pools.

"It's got a swim-up bar. And I think that waterfall is actually a slide."

"No kids."

"One of the advantages of an adult resort. And it's all-inclusive. You want a drink, they bring it to you. You can eat anywhere. The only thing they charge extra for is deep-sea fishing. Basically, you want it, you got it."

She looked at him. "I want a whole lot."

"Then we're in the right place."

Her smile lingered in his mind's eye as she turned back to the scenery. He, on the other hand, had to figure out a way to stay calm. Cool. As if he didn't want to jump her the moment they were in the bungalow. Hell, as if he didn't want to do it right this second.

What the hell had she been thinking when she'd e-mailed him that picture? It didn't come close to what she really looked like. Jeez, she'd caught him completely off guard. Dammit.

The woman was beautiful. She had long, really thick, almost black hair. It framed her face, and oh man, what a face. Dark brows, dark lashes and dark eyes. Pale, delicate skin. The contrast alone was worthy of epic poems.

She was taller than he'd expected, and he could see that all that yoga she talked about had paid off. Again, a mixture. Lean lines with fascinating curves just where they should be.

He couldn't blow this. He hadn't invited her to sexapalooza. In fact, he'd gone to a lot of trouble and expense to make sure she felt completely at ease. But it was clear that if she didn't want to sleep with him, he'd have to kill himself.

"Oh, God," she said.

He followed her gaze to the first clear view of the beach. "This is nothing," he said. "Wait till we get to the other side of the island. There's a huge lagoon. And we have a lot more privacy where we're staying."

"Oh, really?"

He nodded, wanting this part to be over already. It was awkward, the first steps of a new dance. He wanted it to be like when they were online. He could speed things up, take her right to the bungalow, but he'd promised her a tour, and she should have it. There was so much to do here, and even though he'd like to keep her to himself, this was her vacation.

Meg turned to him. "Can I ask you a question?"

"Anything."

"What made you look for the island in the first place?"

"Aside from our fabulous New Year's Eve conversation?"

"Yeah. Aside from that."

He eased the cart around a few trees and toward the

spa. The jungle was thicker here, and he thanked the timing gods that they'd made the trip in February, when the air was perfectly warm, but not too humid to breathe without a snorkel. "You weren't home," he said.

"Ah. Well, that clears everything up. Thanks."

"It's true." God, he was glad she was as sarcastic live as she was online. "You weren't home one night and I'd already written my column about the damn environmental bill I told you about. That idiot Thompson was just spoiling for me to say something that would upset—"

"Alex."

He knew that tone, despite never having heard it before in his life. He had a tendency to get caught up in tangents, even on the computer, and Meg rarely let him get away with it. And now he could put the voice with the sentiment.

It seemed absurd that they'd never talked before. That this was their first meeting. On the other hand, why sit in the frying pan when you can jump right into the fire? "Right. I was seriously thinking about relocation at the time, and I figured an island worked for Gauguin, so why not me? So I surfed the web, and then I came across this island, and it was so much like what we'd talked about that, you know."

"That you decided to spend an absurd amount of money so that we could meet here."

"Basically, yeah. There's the spa." He pointed. "That whole building."

"Is that your way of distracting me from follow-up questions?" she asked.

"No, that's my way of saying there's the spa."

She looked at him. And damn if he didn't recognize that look, too. Yeah, he'd never seen her, except for that surprisingly unflattering picture, but nonetheless.

"And about the questions. I told you. You can ask anything. I have no secrets," he said.

"None?"

"Maybe one."

"Which, of course, I'm going to have to get out of you before our time here is through," Meg teased.

"Go for it."

She grinned, then turned her attention to the spa.

The building was white, like the hotel, and it reminded him of the Greek Isles. Columns, open architecture, stark. A beautiful setting with ample views of the lush vegetation and the ocean. There were also some tents on the outskirts, more Roman than Greek, which were closed to their view. "Those are massage tents."

Meg sighed. "I've dreamed of this. A real massage where I don't have to think, or move, or do anything but make moany noises."

"We can sign up right now."

"Yes, please."

He found the entrance and parked the cart under a nearby tree. Meg climbed out and he followed her up a series of marble steps, between two columns and into a spacious lobby. He hadn't been to a lot of spas, but he'd read about this one, and it was supposed to be one of the best in the world.

A lovely older woman with silver hair smiled at them as they approached the marble desk. "How can I help you?"

"I'd like to get a massage, please," Meg said.

"Of course. We have a four-handed massage, with two therapists working on your body at the same time. Aromatherapy, of course, using some of the fruits and oils unique to the Caribbean. We have reflexology, Swedish massage, hot stone massage, a sports massage tailored to your needs, and of course, our famous couples massage."

"Okay," Meg said. "I'll take one of each."

The woman smiled. "How would you like me to book them?"

"I was kidding. I want them all, but I'll take two—how's that?"

"Whatever we can do to make your stay more relaxing. There are also hydrotherapy sessions, seaweed baths, mud baths, and a mineral salt bath."

"Now that's just being mean."

Alex touched Meg's arm, wanting to give her all those treatments himself. "Anything you want."

"I can't decide. Do you have a brochure?"

"Naturally," she said, handing her the folded chart. "But keep in mind you need to give us some advance notice. What I can do is put you down on our wait list, and notify you when we have an opening."

"That would be wonderful."

While Meg wrote down her name and how long she'd be staying, Alex studied the picture that dominated the wall across from the desk. Maybe he was nuts, but it looked like a Monet. Or a Manet. He could never get them straight. Whichever, it looked like something that belonged in a museum. With the blues and greens and soft lilypads, it was as tranquil as the building, as the breeze.

Meg thanked the receptionist, and they turned to leave. She walked slowly, sniffing the air as she walked. "It's amazing."

"What?"

"The ocean scent. It's all over the island. Everywhere."

"I'm used to the East Coast waters, and I don't remember this smell at all."

"I don't think it's like the California beaches, either. Maybe Catalina, but not quite. It's like the ocean mixed with flowers somehow. I wish I could bottle it and take it home with me."

"If I could get that for you, I would."

She stopped, smiled at him. "This is the best present ever. You know that, right?"

"I hope so." He waited, thinking maybe this would turn into a moment. The thought of kissing her was right there, urging him to move, but he held back. The first kiss was going to have to be her call. After that all bets were off. It wasn't easy, but it was right. He had to wait.

The way she hesitated made him think that she was considering the options. But she didn't lean forward. All she did was smile. It was enough. For now, at least.

"Where do we sign up for the other stuff?"

"Back at the hotel."

"Should we do that now? I'm just thinking the place is pretty crowded…"

"Absolutely. Let's go."

They walked together, matching rhythms as they went down the steps. Once they were in the cart, he turned around and back to the hotel. It was a little trickier to find a place to put the cart, but after driving a few minutes, he found a space. The crowds here made him glad he'd gotten the bungalow, where it was quiet and empty and far away from all these adoring couples.

The entrance to the hotel was even more ornate than the spa facilities. Big marble steps again, but this time there was a fountain that greeted them just before the open front doors. He'd been to Italy several times and he recognized the fountain. It was a smaller version of the Trevi. When they reached the edge, he looked down and found the bottom glittering with coins of all kinds.

"It's like that movie," Meg said.

"Right. Legend has it that if you toss a coin into the fountain, you're destined to come back."

"My wallet's in the cart."

He dug a quarter from his pocket. "Use this one."

"Do I have to do something special? Say any magic words?"

He shook his head. "I don't think so. Maybe turn around and toss it over your shoulder."

"And make a wish?"

"Sure, why not."

She did exactly that. Turned and closed her eyes. He could tell she was getting detailed about the wish, because it took some time, but eventually, the coin went over her shoulder and plopped into the water.

When she opened her eyes again, they were filled with pleasure. If nothing else came of this impromptu getaway, at least he'd given her this. A chance to escape from her brutal work schedule, a way to relax and just take it easy.

"Oh, the hell with it," he said, coming up with another quarter. He turned his back on the fountain, wished in no uncertain terms that the next few days would be filled with a lot more than frolicking in the sand and getting massages from strangers. He didn't open his eyes until he heard the coin splash down.

Meg seemed to think that was funny, which was okay with him. Damn, her laugh was great. But enough of wishing. He wanted to do the sign-up thing so he could take her to the bungalow.

He bowed toward the door. "After you."

Tugging him by the shirt, she led the way, but they both slowed as they went inside. He'd heard about the decor here, and the lobby, more than anything else, told him the tales were true.

The interior was huge and elegant. The furniture was mostly rattan, and a dozen huge plantation ceiling fans made it feel like outdoors. Between the couches were glass-topped tables, most of them with large tropical flower arrangements. Like the spa, the art was all Impressionist paintings, damn good ones. If they were prints, they were the best he'd ever seen. If they were real, he couldn't imagine the kind of security they'd need.

"I think that's where we need to go."

She was pointing at the concierge desk, which had a big Activities banner across the front. A nice-looking woman on the phone smiled at them and held out a clipboard.

Meg took it, and him, to a nearby couch. Alex sat, and then she sat. Close. Really close. Jesus, this was bad. This was really bad. He was way too aware of how much he wanted her, and it had been what, an hour? He could not go there. Not yet. There was time. Now if he could only convince his dick that it should chill.

"Wow, this is a lot of stuff."

He looked at the list as she filled in their names. All major groups were included, from windsurfing to climbing a rock wall.

"Jet Skis. Cool."

He could do Jet Skis. Anybody could do Jet Skis, right? "Great. Mark that one."

"And scuba, of course," she said.

"Uh, yeah. Sure."

Meg turned to him. "Are you certified?"

"Not exactly, no."

"I see."

"I've watched reruns of *Sea Hunt* on *Nick at Nite*. Does that count?"

She grinned.

It wouldn't do any good to be embarrassed. In fact, it was stupid, but he couldn't help it. He wanted her to think he was the alpha male. All buff and strong and able to slay the woolly mammoth. Unfortunately, what he was really good at was conjugating verbs.

"What else?" she asked.

He looked down the list. "Volleyball?"

"I haven't played since high school, but I really liked it. Let's do it." Her comment was punctuated by an audible tummy gurgle. Meg blushed, squinted her eyes.

"Okay, next on the tour will be food, yes?"

"Probably a good thing. The last food I had was hours and hours ago."

"All right. Anything else you want to play?"

She looked at him as if he was going to slap her hand away from the cookie jar. "Do I have to decide it all right now?"

"No, you don't. You don't have to do a damn thing you don't want to. Vacation, remember? All fun, all the time."

"Good. Let's get fed, and then…" She hesitated.

"Yes?"

"Then you can take me to the bungalow."

MEG SAT AT THE LITTLE table, waiting for Alex to come back with their food. She'd ordered too much, but screw it, she was starving. Besides, everything smelled like heaven, and she was a fiend for fish tacos.

She looked behind her. There he stood, chatting with some tall cowboy guy, looking very fine and a wee bit impatient.

Meg was a lot of things, but dense wasn't one of them. The vibes were there between her and Alex. Oh, yeah. And they definitely weren't one-sided. She'd known back in L.A. that she was attracted to him, especially after seeing that one picture. But she'd had no idea she'd want him this much.

Everything from his voice to the crinkle of his eyes when he smiled hit her where it counted. Yeah, it probably didn't help that she hadn't had sex since the Ice Age, but that wasn't the only thing going on.

The problem was that she had no clue what to do. Should she just pounce on him? Get the booty out of the way up front, and hope the spark built? While it was a fine idea, she wasn't sure she could do it. It wasn't her style. Not that she had an actual style, but boinking after an hour and a half wasn't close. So how long was long enough? Four hours? Five?

Of course, if she counted all the online time they'd shared, she'd actually known him a year, which by anyone's standards was more than enough time.

It just didn't *feel* like a year.

If they'd said the exact same words to each other over a computer, she'd have been relaxed and cool as a cucumber. In person, not so much.

She wanted that comfort level back, and something told her it wasn't going to happen in bed. It needed to happen when they were talking, going about the day. Then the bedroom thing would happen naturally. At least, that was her present theory. She reserved the right to change her mind whenever.

She turned back around. He'd be here soon, bearing food and drink, which was good. More talk had to be a step in the right direction.

In the meantime, she could look at the gorgeous view. The ocean wasn't very far away. She had no sense of distance or direction, so she couldn't say exactly how far, just that she could walk it in about five minutes. Alex had scored them a table right on the edge of the deck. She could almost forget that every other table was occupied with couples. Couples who touched. A lot. Kissing was also high on the agenda, with groping tailing by a hair.

It made her discomfort with Alex more acute, and looking at the ocean the best alternative.

God, it was stunning. She'd only seen pictures, and

none of those had even hinted at how it would feel to actually be on that white sand, to smell that orgasmic scent. Even the breeze was something new. Slightly moist, a little salty, it lifted her hair and skimmed every available bare spot.

It would feel luscious to be nude here. To feel it all over.

A shadow on the table made her jump, and she turned to find Alex with a tray. She removed plates, napkins, forks, drinks. Then he put the tray away and came to sit next to her.

"This looks incredible," she said, pulling her plate close.

He grabbed one of his tacos and bit into it with gusto.

She grinned and took a bite of her own. When she'd swallowed, she said, "Ambrosial."

He nodded, but was too busy eating to respond.

Which was just fine. Sitting in the warm air, listening to distant metal drums, feeling the breeze and eating fantastic fish tacos, she felt something inside downshift.

She might not jump him in the next ten minutes or so, but that whole four-hour wait was beginning to feel a mite excessive.

3

"OH, ALEX. IT'S…"

He grinned as he drove their cart to a clearing that overlooked their beach, one he'd scoped out before she'd gotten there. Her reaction was exactly how he'd pictured it. Better. Her hand had gone to her chest—flat palm just under the sweet spot on her neck. It was a nice hand. No jewelry. Her short nails were neat and painted the palest pink.

"It's gorgeous," she said, scanning the magnificent vista.

"Wait till you see inside."

She turned to him again. "You were thinking about relocating?"

"View now. Questions later."

"Promise?" she said.

"There's a phone but you don't have to use it. There's no TV. And I don't think we can fill five whole days with scuba diving, so yeah. I promise."

"I plan to be unbelievably intrusive. Rudely so," she said.

"As long as we're talking quid pro quo," he said, thinking of all kinds of questions he'd like to ask her.

"Hmm."

"What's the worst that can happen?" he asked.

She put her hand on his arm. "You must stop that immediately."

"What?"

"Asking me about the worst that can happen. I know it works for you. You say it, and in your head, the worst can't possibly happen, because you've said the magic words. But they're not magic for me. I do think about the worst, and I don't just go for a quick visit. I linger. I buy new drapes."

"Okay. Consider it done." He'd never thought about that phrase, although he knew he used it often. For him, it was a pressure release. More of a saying than a practice. But clearly, for Meg it meant a lot more.

"Really?" she asked, her brows raising in surprise.

He nodded. "The last thing I want to do is make you uncomfortable, and that's the truth, too."

She laughed.

"Now what?" he said.

"What I just said. What you just said."

"That was funny?" Alex asked, sounding surprised.

"No. I don't do that," Meg stated.

"Talk?"

"No. Put it out there. Not until I know someone really well, and most of the time not even then. But we've been together for two hours, and I said what I meant. And," she said, leaning toward him, widening those beautiful eyes, "nothing horrible happened."

He looked at her so long he almost crashed into a

palm tree. But once they were steady on the path again, he nodded. "You know what?"

"What?" she asked.

"This is gonna be interesting."

THE BUNGALOW WAS something out of a dream. Thatched roof, wooden steps leading up to a balcony. The ocean as pure and clear as if it had just been made.

With the scented breeze nudging her hair, teasing her skin, she let Alex tackle her big suitcase while she grabbed her small one. Her sandals clicked on the boardwalk as she stared down into the water, watching a little something dart behind a slightly bigger something.

When she stepped up onto the balcony, she was torn between seeing what treats lay inside and just standing there breathless with wonder.

It was the brush of his hand on the small of her back that made her decision, and after a shiver of sheer happiness, she went the rest of the way inside.

"Oh, my God," she said.

His chuckle, rumbling, deep, was the perfect first sound in this perfect paradise. Shiny, geometric patterns of wood made up the floor and the walls. The staircase to the loft was made of thicker wood, like flattened tree branches. Windows opened to the ocean, to the white sand.

Then there was the bed. It was right out of a Humphrey Bogart movie, complete with white mosquito netting and lush white pillows on top of an obscenely thick comforter. The couch, a rattan affair with thick blue cushions, looked inviting and comfy, and everything, everything smelled of the sea.

"You like?" he asked.

She turned. Alex stood with his arms across his chest, like the inventor of the wheel. His dark brows lifted and his teasing lips blossomed into a full-out, take-no-prisoners grin. She couldn't grin any harder herself. Her cheeks actually ached from the attempt. "It's heaven."

He rose up on the balls of his feet. "Damn straight."

How could she resist? He couldn't even stay on the ground, he was so pleased. She walked right up to him, looked into eyes that were dark blue, not brown, and touched his cheek with her fingertips. "It's hard to believe it's real."

"Maybe it's not. Maybe it's still New Year's Eve and we're still drunk."

"That would explain so much," Meg said, leaning in. And then her lips met his. Softly. Learning. Slightly parted.

His breath snuck inside, and it was sweet and a little minty. She felt his hand slip to her waist, but there was no pressure, just contact.

She moved closer, parting her lips. He followed her lead, not forcing anything. Until she licked his bottom lip. Then he pulled her tight against him, from breast to thigh, and the kiss went from sweet to hot in one blazing second.

Meg froze. Just…froze.

Alex, to his credit, backed off immediately. Even more to his credit, he didn't seem the least freaked that she'd freaked. He smiled, tilted his head to the right, but he only said, "Why don't you get unpacked? Check out the room, and don't forget to look at the guest services book. Remember," he added pointedly, "anything you want, anytime you want it."

"Thanks, Alex," she said. She went to her big suit-case and hauled it up to the bed. "Where will you be?"

He gestured upstairs. "Figured I'd put on some trunks. Get ready for some fun on the beach. Come back down when you're done."

She watched him walk up the wooden staircase, her gaze moving down from his shoulders to his waist, to his long legs. As soon as he disappeared, she sat down with a whuff.

The kiss had gobsmacked her in a major way. A nor-mal person would have been pleased. Would have wanted more. Would have shouted yippee from the roof. But no. Not her.

It hadn't been *that* long, had it? She'd gone out just last…

Spring.

God, she was such an incredible loser. Instead of finding herself a nice, hunky guy to share her bed, what did she do? Slept with a three-legged Labrador retriever and a blind cat. Yeah. That was healthy.

The good news was she still had time to get her act together. Alex didn't seem upset, or even that surprised, which worked in her favor. The bad news was, what the hell was her problem?

She stood and unzipped her suitcase, amused at how much she'd packed. She could have fit the necessary clothing in her overnight case. She wouldn't be need-ing her jeans, or much of anything but her bathing suits and sundresses.

It made putting things away a lot easier. All her makeup, which she didn't even think she'd use, was in one case. Her hairbrush and dryer, another. And then there was the large, economy box of condoms she'd picked up in a haze of optimism.

Time. That's all she needed. Time to feel as if the man in the bungalow was the same man she liked so much. That she knew so well.

That knew her.

Holy crap, she'd told him so much about herself.

She felt her cheeks fill with heat. They hadn't actually had cyber sex. Not really. But the man definitely had a starring role in a lot of her fantasies.

Which they'd discussed. In detail.

Not him, per se, but the fantasies? Oh, yeah.

She knew he liked things intense. That he preferred women who gave as good as they got. That he was a very oral kind of guy. And that he had a thing for white panties.

He knew that her tastes weren't exactly vanilla.

She looked at the box of condoms. She should have wished for courage at that fountain.

ALEX SPLASHED MORE WATER on his face, then leaned on his arms while he dripped into the sink.

He was in trouble. The kind that reminded him of what it had been like to be seventeen. It had sucked. He'd had no control over his dick, he'd been tongue-tied and stupid, and he'd stuttered when he was around women. Make that any woman. Except his mother and his aunt Esther. Theoretically, he'd outgrown that stage of development.

He raised his gaze to the beveled mirror. He wasn't a kid anymore, not by a long shot. He was a professional. Maybe that should be ex-professional, but still. He'd won prizes. So why was he feeling like... Like he was seventeen again?

He was pretty damn sure he hadn't been a jerk with her. Yeah, he'd kissed her, but she started it.

Oh, yeah. Mature. That was him all over.

They had five days. Five days to talk, to let her feel comfortable with him, to get to know each other. But damn, he wanted her.

She knew things about him that he'd never told anyone. Not even Ellen. And he'd been in love with Ellen. At least, he used to think so.

Now, he wasn't sure. About Ellen, about his work, about his whole goddamn life. What he was sure about was this. Bringing Meg here. Getting away from everything that screwed with both their heads.

And he'd do whatever it took to make sure that it went perfectly. Even if that meant he'd have to suffer.

He laughed at himself. Loudly. Suffer? Please. He was in paradise with a gorgeous woman who got his jokes. Even if they never...

Ah, bullshit. She wanted him. She just didn't know it yet.

"What's so funny?" she asked softly.

He turned, and there she was. He hadn't even heard her come upstairs. She'd pulled her glorious mane back into a loose ponytail, which made her look, however improbably, more beautiful. She had this flimsy little scarf thing on that couldn't hide the itsy-bitsy bikini underneath.

Seventeen was generous. He was all the way back at the first day of puberty. "What?"

"You were laughing. I heard you down the stairs."

"Remembering an old joke," he said, lame as that was.

"I'd like to hear it," she persisted.

"You're too young, and we need to go to the beach," he said, not knowing what else to say.

"A moral imperative?"

"I believe so, yes."

"Then I suggest you get out of those jeans," she teased.

Alex blinked. Then kicked the bathroom door shut.

MEG LOOKED AROUND the loft, searching for clues. She ran her hand down her thigh as she wandered to his bed. Actually, the bedside table. There was a book there, facedown, and she had to pick it up, see what he was reading. *Up Country* by Nelson DeMille. She liked DeMille, but she hadn't known Alex did.

What she did know was his taste in music. Jazz. Obscure jazz, on vinyl, to be precise. It was how they'd met.

Next to the book was a portable CD player, and when she flipped it open, she smiled. Art Tatum. She had this exact LP, and they'd listened to it together, him in D.C., her in L.A., while they'd typed to each other.

Her father had been a collector. He'd loved the big bands. There were rare days, days when he was actually home, that she'd walk into the living room to find the music blaring on their ancient hi-fi, and her parents doing the Lindy Hop, with wide, bright smiles on their faces.

She'd first learned to dance by standing on her father's shoes as he'd moved her around the room. Jazz had been her childhood soundtrack, and hearing certain songs, even now, brought her right back to the moments, large and small, of growing up with her slightly nutty folks.

After her father died, leaving her his practice, she'd gone back to that old love. She'd searched for others who shared the passion. That's where she'd first run into Alex. In a chat room for jazz fans.

He was a collector also, and at first, their conversations had been exclusively jazz-centric. He wasn't so much into the big bands as he was the singers. Billie Holiday. Cab Calloway. But they'd understood each other, right from the get-go. They had this shared language, which made the conversations flow.

Then they started chatting about other things. He lived such an interesting life. As a columnist for the *Washington Post*, he was at the cutting edge of politics, and damn, he wasn't afraid to say what he felt. That was one of the things she liked most about him. She never had to wonder.

Her life seemed so mundane in comparison, but he always wanted to hear her stories. Her practice was more like the veterinarians of old, or at least of small towns. She treated everything from hamsters to llamas. On her mountain, an enclave of ex-hippies and old coots, there was every kind of creature, and she was the only vet. The only one they trusted, at least. Because her beloved father had trusted her, and that was sacrosanct.

She checked Alex's bathroom door. It was still shut, and she wondered what the hell was taking him so long. All he had to do was put on some trunks. Then she turned back, wondering if she dared open the drawer. It was a pretty nosy thing to do. She wouldn't care for it one bit if he invaded her space like that. But then, she'd never said she was fair.

She did it. She opened the drawer really carefully, even knowing the door behind her could open the next second. And she burst out laughing.

Condoms. The exact same brand that she'd put in the exact same drawer next to her bed.

She covered her mouth to muffle the sound when the door opened behind her. Spinning around, she shoved the drawer closed with her hip and tried to look innocent.

"What?" he asked.

"What?" she asked back.

"You're blushing."

"I'm just warm."

He walked toward her slowly, studying her far too intently. "I think your nose just grew, Pinocchio."

"I was snooping. Are you happy now?"

He nodded, but his scrutiny didn't end. "And what did you learn?"

"That you like DeMille. And Tatum."

"Art or O'Neil?"

She laughed, moving away from the drawer. "How about that walk on the beach?"

He smiled back, and although they'd only met that afternoon, she knew without a doubt that he knew she'd peeked in the drawer. Which was only fair, she supposed.

"Did you remember your sunscreen?"

"Yes, in fact, I did," she said.

"Good. I wouldn't want that beautiful nose to burn."

Her fingers went to said nose in a moment of adolescent shyness.

He winked at her, and her hand moved from her nose to her tummy, which had gone all mushy. Then he led her down the stairs, through the bungalow, then onto the incredible white sand.

She hadn't bothered with shoes, because, why? And the feel of the sand under her feet was unlike anything she'd experienced before. She was used to Southern California beaches, where the water was cold, the sand dirty, and you had to watch every step because you never knew where a pop top was hiding.

This was pristine and soft. The water was perfect, not as warm as the air, but not too chilly. "Oh, man, this is—"

"The farthest thing from Washington, D.C., I could think of."

"No, I think that would be Antarctica, but hey, this works, too," she said.

"You're cute. Anybody ever tell you that?" Alex quipped.

"And yet, somehow, I can't hear it enough."

His grin was as warm as the sunshine as they wandered down the beach. There were birds in the distance, and although she couldn't see them, she imagined exotic plumage and long beaks, all courtesy of the Discovery Channel and, in the distant past, her own studies. She should have been used to palm trees, but these were actual natives, not like the ones in L.A., and she had to fight back the urge to touch every one.

She turned to the other thing she wanted to touch, letting her gaze wander over his chest. Not perfect—no six-pack there—but it was nice. Strong. And so were the thighs beneath his blue trunks. "So why did you really do this?"

"Birthday present," he said quickly.

"No, that was the excuse. What's going on?" she asked.

He kicked some sand and increased the distance between them by a hair. "Things have been…interesting with work."

"Interesting as in the old Chinese curse?"

He smiled, nodded. "I used to love waking up in the morning. Seriously. I couldn't get enough. Nothing mattered except the work. This was even before the column, when I was learning the ropes at the *Post*. Everything was exciting and challenging, and I was on the side of the White Hats for truth, justice and the American way."

"And now?"

"Haven't you heard? Gray is the new white. And my hat's become a bit tarnished."

"Oh." She tried to see his eyes, but he was assiduously studying the sand. "Care to elaborate?"

"Not really," he said.

"Is it just work? Or are things not peachy in your personal life, either?" she asked.

"What personal life?"

"Ah, that's a tune I know by heart," she said, sighing. "Honey, you wrote the music."

She stopped. It took him a minute to realize that she wasn't next to him, but then he came back.

"We've chatted pretty much every night for eons, talked about everything from Nietzsche to your obsession with white panties, and this is the first time I'm hearing you're unhappy with your work?" she said.

He shrugged.

"But your column is doing so well."

He looked at her with such troubled eyes that she hardly knew what to do. "Let's go swimming," he suggested.

She reached to pull off her cover-up. "We didn't bring towels."

"Oh. Not good. You go on in. I'll be right back."

"Okay, thanks."

He hesitated, and she wasn't quite sure why. That look was still in his eyes, that combination of hope and despair that made her want to hold him. With a slight shake of his head, he turned back to the bungalow, jogging easily through the sand.

Just yesterday she'd told herself over and over that she knew this man. That she'd spent a year getting to know him. They'd shared secrets. Big ones. And she didn't know something as huge as his unhappiness with his work?

What else didn't she know?

She tossed her cover-up to the sand and walked into the surf. The waves brushed her legs and then her thighs. The water was a little chillier than she'd first thought, but nice. She lived an hour from the beach in L.A. and she couldn't remember the last time she'd been in the ocean.

He was right. She had written the book on working too much. It had to stop, or she was going to lose it big time. The only problem was, she didn't know how to stop it.

The first step was to stop thinking about it. To stop thinking altogether. And the best way to do that was to have oodles of hot, sweaty sex. Having seen Alex's super pack o' condoms, she surmised that he needed the exact same thing.

Anesthesia by orgasm.

It worked for her.

4

ALEX GRABBED A COUPLE OF the big towels, both of them vivid with animal prints, and went back out to meet Meg. Thigh-deep in the water, she was as beautiful as anything on the island.

He hadn't expected that. He'd been so used to looking at her picture that she didn't really seem like the same woman.

Not that he was complaining, but it was still a little disconcerting.

Which was how she must be feeling after his confession. He hadn't even planned on telling her. At least not on the first day. She didn't need to be burdened with his crap. It was probably all midlife-crisis bullshit, although he was only thirty-three. And for God's sake, he worked in politics. How could anyone not get caught up in all that power and all that bull? It had crept up on him with amazing stealth. Secrets shared, held close to the vest, but they all came with a price. Nothing earthshaking, nothing to lose sleep over. Until he was buried so deep he could hardly breathe.

Which was why he'd needed to get the hell out. To take his mind off work, off Washington, off anything but one beautiful woman who made him laugh as much as she made him hard.

He jogged through the sand, checking out Meg, checking out the emptiness of the beach, putting two and two together. Although the actuality of doing anything out here, while private, would probably be uncomfortable. Sand had its place, and that was far, far away from all the good body parts.

On the bright side, the bungalows were real close.

Meg turned as he spread out the second towel. She was in up to her waist now. When the waves receded, her hips and thighs came into view.

He wanted to touch her. Everywhere the water touched. He wanted to feel the soft skin between her thighs, trace every curve.

"It's fabulous," she said, waving him in.

He went in, shocked by how cold the water was, but completely unwilling to admit it. Smile firmly in place, he decided this was another reason not to have sex at the beach.

"Is it always this deserted?" she asked.

"No idea. The other bungalows are booked, though. I know, because the only reason I got this one, considering the holiday, was through contacts at the paper. Redskins tickets were involved."

She grinned as she dunked a little deeper into the water. "I'm glad you didn't say blackmail, because I doubt very much I would have cared."

"Confessions of wickedness so early in the week? Excellent."

She splashed him and the shock of the water threatened his manly countenance. He managed to hold it together somehow. Especially with Meg as a reward.

"The water is so clear. I can't even imagine how good the snorkeling's going to be," she said.

Should he tell her he'd never been snorkeling? Or on Jet Skis? Or gone windsurfing? That his experience with large bodies of water consisted of flying over them at thirty-five thousand feet? And was there any cool way of casually mentioning that he played a mean game of one-on-one at his local park?

He decided to show, not tell, so he took three long strides, then dived into the water. Tensing from the cold, he swam until he got more accustomed, which was just long enough so that he gasped for breath when he shot up.

Actually, he felt pretty damn good. Which had more to do with Meg than with the ocean, but the ocean didn't hurt.

She was laughing. What a sight it was. Broad laughter. Laughter that involved every part of her, and he chalked up another one for the good guys. He knew she didn't laugh like this often. Her life was one problem after another, one horse, one llama, one cat, then the next. Always on call, never enough help. Never enough rest because the phone might ring.

They both needed to be here. And they both needed to get the hell over whatever awkwardness they felt, and get down to it.

He was going to make sure that by the time Meg Becker got back on the plane, she'd be the most sexually satisfied woman who ever lived.

If he felt damn good along the way, so much the better.

As he watched her, as the waves knocked him in the ass with soothing regularity and the sun warmed his chest, her laughter stilled. She rocked with the same rhythm, from the same waves. The joy was still there in her eyes, but something else was there, too.

Curiosity. Desire. But still, that bit of hesitation. They knew each other and they didn't. The only cure was getting close, letting down the walls. Telling the truth.

He wasn't used to that. Not that he lied all the time, but he'd learned to be very selective about what he said to whom. It was all about omission in his line of work. Getting the other person to reveal too much, while he revealed nothing at all.

Which was great when he interviewed a congressman, but counterproductive in the ocean with the woman he hoped to sleep with until they both cried uncle. "I was thinking about walking to the hotel tonight. Getting some dinner, checking out the disco. What do you think?"

"I think yes," she said. "But I'm going to need a nap before that. I've been up since dawn."

"Sounds like a plan. Now quit being such a wuss and let's do some real swimming," he said.

"Who you callin' a wuss?" she asked, hands on her perfect hips.

"If the shoe fits."

She gave him the evil eye seconds before she dived sleekly into the water. He watched her glide along, the ocean so clear it was like glass. She stopped when she was just behind him, and as he turned, she rose from the sea.

Glistening, dripping, beautiful. Even though she was

close enough to touch, he resisted. Too soon, and too much, and she'd been traveling since last night. He wanted her to be comfortable and willing. There was time enough. If he could last. Which wasn't looking so good at the moment.

He yawned widely. Nap. Yep, that would be good. The privacy wouldn't hurt, either.

"Now who's the wuss?"

"You're the one who brought up sleep," he said.

She grinned as she squeezed the seawater from her long ponytail. "Okay, naps it is. Right after we finish swimming."

"Finish?"

"We've just gotten wet. Come on, you can't tell me you're done already," she teased.

"Me? Nah. I'm raring to go."

She grinned. "Raring, huh?"

"If I had an engine, it would be revving," he said.

"You're completely full of it, aren't you?"

"What gave it away?"

"The way you keep inching toward the shore was my first clue," she said.

"Busted."

"We've got days to swim. Let's go."

He grabbed her arm as she turned. "No, no. Swimming is good. Seriously. I just haven't been in the ocean much. Did you know it was salty?"

That made her laugh. Which was a good thing. "Okay, we'll swim. For a little while."

"Deal," he said.

"Then we nap," she stated.

"Also a deal," he said.

"But not for long. An hour, tops. There's too much I want to do today."

He nodded his assent to that, too. Then he dived into the water once more. This time was better. Especially when she shimmied up next to him. God, how she moved in the water. She flowed as if she was born to it, all grace and clean lines. He could watch her forever.

THEY WALKED BACK to the bungalow wrapped in the beach towels. At the door, Meg kissed him. Nothing monumental, just a brush of lips on lips and a quick retreat. It was a start.

Although he ached for more, he kept his cool. "Are you sure an hour's going to be enough? Sleep, I mean."

She nodded. "There's too much I want to see. I'll sleep in tomorrow."

"Okay, then."

She hesitated, a little crease forming between her eyebrows.

Alex waited, but she simply shook her head and walked inside. He hung his towel on the deck railing and followed her, but headed right for the stairs. The loft was cool, even more so when he stripped off his trunks. Tempted to leave them on the floor, he instead went to the bathroom, rinsed out the saltwater and hung them over the shower stall. Although the idea of just falling into bed was incredibly tempting, he turned on the water in the shower. Might as well go to sleep clean. Besides, the shower was an excellent place to take care of some important business, especially considering she was just downstairs.

He got inside, letting the heat soak into his muscles. Eyes closed, he thought about her as his hand went to his thickening cock. He rubbed lightly with his forefinger and thumb, but teasing wasn't going to cut it. Not with the possibilities of what lay ahead, a jumble of erotic pictures flashing one after the other in his tired head.

One image surfaced and stuck. It was from a conversation they'd had ages ago. He'd accused her of being a prude for some reason he could no longer recall, and she'd laughed at him. Of course it was typed, but he could tell it was real. Then the line came that had been his companion until the wee hours of that morning: I'll admit I haven't had the most experience in the world, but there's not much I wouldn't be willing to try.

If she'd told the truth, if she truly was as adventurous as she claimed, then this week could be the most exciting of his life. The things he wanted to do to her. With her.

The images grew more vivid, and okay, so maybe the whole white panties thing was an obsession, but he'd feel bad about that later. For now, it was Meg and she was naked, and holy shit.

His balls tightened and his head hit the shower stall as he shot, pure and hard, and Jesus, what was it going to be like when he was actually with the real, live woman?

Slumping against the cold tile wall, he waited until his legs were steady, then he washed, wondering where he was going to get the patience to let her call the shots. Because, dammit, he wasn't going to screw this up.

Whatever happened here on the island, the friendship had to be maintained. Nothing, not even his untrustworthy cock, was going to get in the way.

MEG TURNED OVER, trying to find the perfect spot on the luxuriously soft bed. She was exhausted, especially after her swim, but she couldn't get her mind to shut the hell up.

All she could think of was what was going to happen over the next few days. Not the fun-time activities at the hotel or in the water, but between the sheets.

She'd liked Alex from their first conversation online. He'd been funny and sweet, and he knew how to spell. It was incredibly snobby, she knew, but if someone couldn't spell or had lousy grammar, she simply couldn't get into any kind of lengthy discussion. That he was a writer had come as no surprise.

As they'd gotten to know each other, they'd talked about everything, not just jazz, and she'd found his opinions erudite, witty and compelling. Not that she'd agreed with everything he'd said, but he'd kept her on her toes.

It reminded her of college, and her classes in philosophy, the discussions at the dorm that went way into the night, when the topics ran the gamut from the social significance of *The Simpsons* to the emerging European Union.

While Meg didn't regret her decision to become a vet, she often wondered what her world would have been like if she'd followed another path. She'd thought about being a teacher. Her love of the language had begun early in life, and her hunger for books had never abated. Part of what killed her about her situation on the mountain was that she rarely had time to read.

Chatting with Alex had given her a great deal of the stimulation she needed, in addition to doing something books couldn't—he kept her awake. In the past few years, every time she opened a book, she'd fall asleep by page ten. It wasn't fair.

She shifted again, this time plumping the pillow. Dammit, she needed this nap. Tonight was going to be wonderful, but not if she couldn't keep her eyes open. Knowing he was just upstairs wasn't helping.

Meg sighed. She knew a surefire way of getting some peace. Not that it was unpleasant, but she'd wanted this week to be about real, live sex, not vibrator sex. She'd brought her vibe along just in case, but now that she'd met Alex…

Which kind of brought up the next big topic. If she jumped him before dinner would he get the wrong impression? The last thing she wanted him to think was that she was a tramp. On the other hand, the subtext for the whole trip was that they were going to hump like bunnies, so what was the big deal?

She opened the bedside drawer, reached behind the condoms and found her virtually silent bed buddy, then got comfy again. He'd said an hour. He wouldn't surprise her, and even if he wasn't asleep, he couldn't see her bed from the loft.

She held her breath for a moment, straining to hear if he was moving around upstairs. Nothing. At least not from the loft. But there were definitely sounds, and they weren't tropical birds.

A woman's voice came through Meg's window. An argument, from the sound of it. Meg couldn't hear the other side; the woman must be standing near an open window.

It wasn't the fantasy soundtrack of Meg's dreams, but it wasn't so loud she couldn't deal with it. It did make her feel bad that anyone could fight in such a wonderful place. She turned to the small clock radio on the nightstand and turned it on to what was evidently the only station on the island. Instrumental music of the tropical kind. It did the trick. She settled back on her pillow, closed her eyes and went straight for the good stuff.

A bounty of fantasies awaited, and all of them took place in paradise with the man sleeping upstairs. The exotic won out over the mundane, and she pictured them in a cove, with the ocean as a melody, him taking off her clothes until she stood naked on the pale sand.

The look in his eyes was hungry, ravenous, as if he'd never wanted anyone as much as he wanted her. His touch, oh my. Electric, knowing just where, just how.

Her muscles tightened, her head went back as she tensed, and almost before it had begun, she was there. Gasping, clenching. Letting the orgasm flood through her body like honey, all the while making no noise at all, but thinking, *yes, yes, yes*.

Her eyes closed as sleep descended, so quickly she didn't even bother putting the vibe away. She simply shoved it under the comforter on the other side of the bed, seconds before she was out.

AT FOUR THIRTY-ONE, Alex thought about going downstairs. It might be a bit soon, considering they'd parted at three-thirty, but she'd been very clear about the one-hour thing. The fact that he couldn't think of anything but being with her had nothing to do with it. Okay, it had everything to do with it.

He'd crashed hard and fast after the shower, and awakened surprisingly refreshed. Because they wouldn't be back before dinner, he'd put on jeans and a button-down shirt. He'd thought about wearing trunks instead of shorts but decided if they were going to go swimming tonight, it was going to be somewhere private, and it was going to be naked.

He went to his window and looked out over the ocean. Just staring at that wide expanse of water and sky relaxed him. He thought about his office. It was downstairs, in the back of his town house. There was one window, which overlooked a forlorn little park. It didn't matter because he never looked out. He was a panic writer, always waiting until the last minute to get his column done, and when he wasn't working on the column, he used his laptop either upstairs or on the kitchen table. Mostly, though, he was on the phone or at a restaurant. His contacts were everything. At least, they had been. He doubted he would have any by the time he got back. Which wasn't the end of the world, right? Jesus, he hoped it wouldn't be.

After making sure his wallet was in his pocket, he stood at the top of the stairs, listening for signs that she was up.

He heard footsteps, so he went down. She smiled as she saw him, and the look of her in her snug blue dress, with her hair cascading in waves around her face and onto her shoulders, almost made him groan. God, the dress was strapless, and it emphasized the length of her neck, her toned arms, to say nothing of her long, slender legs.

"I was just coming to get you," she said, her voice filled with excitement. "It's so beautiful out there."

"My thoughts exactly," he said. "A perfect time for a walk to the hotel."

"I brought a wrap. Do you think it'll get much cooler?"

"I don't think so, but this is my first time here, so…"

"You'll keep me warm." With that, she went out. No purse, no wrap, nothing but the woman and the little strapless dress.

He watched as she stepped over to the edge of the balcony, how her dress curved over her ass as she walked. All that stuff about waiting for her to make the first move?

Not gonna happen.

5

"WELL, HELLO THERE."

Alex and Meg turned toward the bungalow just down the boardwalk to find a woman leaning against the railing, her filmy scarf wafting in the breeze. She was in her mid-fifties, and dressed in a bright resort ensemble. Her hair was short, her earrings big, and her smile was a bit too wide.

She pushed off the rail and walked toward them. "I'm Tina Lester," she said, holding out a manicured hand. "I see we're neighbors."

Alex took her hand. "Hi. Alex Rosten. And this is Meg Becker."

Tina smiled at Meg. "How are you enjoying the island?"

"It's great so far," Meg replied. "Haven't been here that long."

"We saw you check in this afternoon. You're going to love it. There's so much beauty and tranquility. So good for the soul."

Meg smiled. "Right."

Tina looked behind her just as a man walked out of their bungalow. He was in a Hawaiian shirt that wasn't too garish, and khaki shorts that showed off his fish-belly-white legs. "And this is Walter. Darling, this is Alex and Meg."

"How you doing?" Walter said, sans smile. He did, however, perk up when his phone rang. He retrieved it from his pants pocket and flipped it open. He turned toward the bungalow and in seconds he was involved in an argument that had him close to a bellow.

Even Alex could tell these two were not on a second honeymoon. He looked to Tina, whose lips had pressed together. She closed her eyes briefly, and when she opened them again, she seemed more resigned than angry, and yet the tension was thicker than the scent of the sea.

Walter turned back to them as he closed his cell phone. He still wasn't smiling, and didn't seem in the least pleased to meet their bungalow mates.

"Hi, Walter," Meg said. "It's nice meeting you. I'm sure we'll run into you again, but please excuse us now. We're late for our spa appointments."

Tina opened her mouth, but Walter spoke first. "Unless you're shopping, you're not likely to run into her. You two have a nice night."

"Thanks," Alex said, hurrying Meg down the stairs. They made it to the path unscathed, clutching each other as if they'd escaped from the lion's den.

He steered her toward the path that would lead them to the hotel. "Whoa. That was interesting."

Meg leaned in close and whispered, "I heard them arguing earlier. I couldn't make out the words, but the tone was clear enough."

"Well, we don't have to socialize. This is our vacation and we can do whatever we want."

"Right," she said, "but just so you know? With the windows open, voices carry."

He tried to remember if he'd said anything while he'd been in the shower. He didn't think so, but maybe he'd groaned or something. Nothing he could do about it now, anyway. He pulled Meg closer with his arm around her waist. "Did you get any sleep?"

"Eventually. Actually, I slept wonderfully once I could finally relax. All this travel and excitement. I'm not used to it."

"How far away is that mountain of yours from the beach?"

"About an hour, but that doesn't mean much. I hardly ever go."

"Yeah. I can see how it would be tough to find the time."

"Rule for tonight," she said. "No talk of work. None at all. Everything else is fair game, but we're on vacation and I don't want to give up even a minute of it."

"Deal," he said, more relieved than he could say. If he could just stop thinking about the chaos he'd left in D.C., he'd be the happiest man on the island.

She looked again at the sea, at the clouds, at the emptiness of the beach. "Wow."

"You can say that again."

"Wow."

He winced. "Okay, you get that one. But only that one."

She laughed, but her expression turned serious as she studied his face. "Tell me about her."

"Her?"

"Ellen."

"Ah. Not much to say. We were together for about eight months. Then she got the job in Paris," he said.

"Weren't you two engaged?" Meg asked.

"I suppose you could say that," he said.

"Did you ask her to marry you?"

"Yeah."

"Trust me, that counts," she said.

"It wasn't as serious as all that. I thought we were good together. She had her own life, I had mine and we met in the middle. It was easy. Neither of us had to do much. It sure as hell wasn't a great romance."

"So it was more an engagement of convenience?" Meg asked.

"That's one way of putting it. I hate dating. I'd rather face a firing squad than start from scratch with a new woman. I'm desperately tired of my story, and I can't remember the last time I was interested in hearing anyone else's. With one notable exception, of course," he said with a smile.

"Thanks, I think."

"Maybe it's because of how we met. I was predisposed in your favor. After all, your taste in music is impeccable."

"I don't think it was because of the way we met. I think it was because of the ground rules," she stated.

They reached a rough-hewn path and turned away from the sea toward the hotel and civilization. His steps slowed. He liked having Meg to himself. Selfish, but true. "What ground rules?" he asked.

"Until your little surprise, there was never any expectation that we'd be more than online friends. No chance the chemistry wouldn't be there, because we weren't going to meet. I never tried to impress you," she said.

"Never?"

"Okay, maybe once or twice, but it's not the same." She tugged at his hand. "You know what I mean. There's the whole mating ritual dance. Everyone does it. I'm severely out of practice, but I vaguely remember the moves. We just talked. Like people."

It was his turn to laugh. "Right. Like people."

"Am I wrong?"

"Nope. I think you're brilliant and astute and you've hit the nail on the head. Which begs the question…" He paused.

"Yes?"

"Have I blown it? Is this little surprise going to wreck it all?"

She stopped walking altogether, pulling him around to face her. "I don't think so. But I'm not sure. This is very new territory."

"Okay," he said slowly. "Let me ask you this. What do you want?"

"World peace?"

"Cute."

"Okay, okay. I'm soft-pedaling here because I don't know that I have an answer," she said.

"You must have some idea," he insisted.

"Aside from enjoying the island?" she asked.

"Yeah."

She didn't answer. Instead, she just shifted so that they were holding hands and started walking again. Not that far ahead, there were people. Couples. Walking, mostly, but two were on bicycles, and there were a few of the golf cart jobs. Everyone seemed young and tan and attractive.

While Alex waited for her to answer he thought about his own expectations. Yeah, he'd wanted to get out of Dodge before the shit hit the fan, but that was secondary. It had cost him a fortune, and he hadn't given the money a second thought. He'd wanted this vacation, and he'd wanted it with Meg. No one else. She'd been a critical part of his entire decision, even though she didn't know it. He intended to thank her in every possible way.

"You know what surprises me most?" she asked.

"What?"

"I figured the moment we met face-to-face it would all be okay. As if we'd known each other for ages. That I'd be completely relaxed, and it would be nothing but easy."

Her grip had tightened and he could tell that while her voice was light, the subject wasn't.

"But…"

"Not that it's been difficult. It's just not what I expected. There's a whole level of not knowing you that I wasn't prepared for. Which is kind of stupid, but there you have it," she said.

He stopped and turned toward her, wanting to see her eyes. "What do you mean?"

"Physically," she said. "Meeting in person changes things. I'm a lot more self-conscious than I anticipated." She lowered her eyes, but only for a moment. "I want you to like me, and up until I decided to come here, I didn't worry about it. I *knew* you liked me," she said.

"Well, I do."

"That's not what I mean," she stated quickly.

"I know that, too."

She frowned. "Do you?"

"I'm astoundingly attracted to you," he said, brushing the side of her face with the back of his hand

"Yeah?"

"Oh, yeah."

"Because I'm here or because I'm me?" she asked.

He had to grin. "Subtle, Meg. Real subtle."

"I'm on an island a gazillion miles from home for five days with a man I've never met before. And you want me to tiptoe?"

"No, no. Not at all. I want honesty. Nothing less," he insisted.

"And still you haven't answered my question," she said.

Alex looked Meg straight in the eye. "You. Because you're you. And because I want to know more. You've been the one thing that's completely right in my life. As soon as I see your name on the computer, I relax. And what's a vacation supposed to be, if not relaxing? So, again, I say, it's you. Just you."

Her smile came slowly, but when it hit, it was a dazzler. "Good answer."

She shifted her weight, leaning forward just enough for her body to touch his. Her breath, sweet and slightly cinnamon, brushed his chin. "Just so you know? I was thinking about our plans for the evening. You know, drinks, dinner, disco."

"Is there a problem?" he asked.

"No, not at all. It sounds great. Almost perfect," she said.

"Almost?" he asked, hoping against hope she was leading to the one thing that would make the night a total hit.

"You forgot about dessert. In the brochure it said the Trade Winds has the best key lime pie ever."

"Ah." He tried his damnedest to keep his disappointment in check. "Lucky for us, our reservations are at that very establishment."

"Excellent."

A couple on a tandem bike rode by and waved. Meg waved back.

Alex just kept thinking about the next four days. There were four nights, too, and now that she'd voiced her reservations, he couldn't possibly press, but with luck…

"Oh, wait," she said, turning back to face him. "Did I mention the whole having sex part?"

His heart thudded as his feet stopped. The last time he'd felt that very sensation was when he'd missed hitting a drunk pedestrian by about eight inches. It had taken him a long time to calm down from that spike of adrenaline. He doubted he would be so quick to recover from this.

"I meant you and me," she said brightly. "In case you were wondering."

"That's good. That's a really fine plan. I can honestly say I'm all in favor of doing each and every one of those things."

She smiled and the breath across his chin came a little more rapidly.

He smiled right back. "However, and this is sim-

ply as a fallback position, not that I *want* to skip any
of those activities, but if things happen and we're
forced to let one or two or four things slide, I do have
a preference."

"Really?" she said.

He nodded. Jesus, he was getting hard. And she was
close enough that if this conversation went on much
longer, she'd be sure to notice. Maybe that wasn't a bad
thing. "Yeah."

"And what would your preference be?" she asked.

"Dinner. That key lime pie sounds great."

She pinched him. Right on the ass. He hadn't even
felt her arm move around to his back. "Ow."

"Tell me you didn't deserve that," she said.

"If I admit culpability, will you stop pinching me?"
he asked.

"I don't know. Do you want me to stop?"

"I'm not sure. Although, if you think about it, there are
other things one could do to show one's displeasure that
wouldn't involve pinching so much as kissing," he teased.

Meg laughed. "You do something naughty, and I'm
supposed to kiss you?"

"I call it gentle correction."

"You're completely full of shit, aren't you?" she said.

"Not about the gentle correction. Oh, yeah."

"I see," she murmured.

"Now I have a question." Alex moved just that tiny
bit closer. Close enough that she would clearly understand his condition. "Why are we standing on this sandy
path, when we have so very many intriguing things to
do tonight?"

She pressed her body into his. "You're suggesting we get it in gear?" she asked.

"I am," he said firmly.

"I'll take it under advisement."

He raised his brows, wanting so much to pull her tighter against him.

"After," she said.

"After what?" he asked.

"This," she whispered, as she rose up to kiss him.

Jesus, it was worth the wait. Her mouth was soft and teased him with possibilities. How in hell was he supposed to get through dinner, dessert, dancing? How was he supposed to get through the next three minutes?

When she pulled back, her face was flushed a sexy pink, her lips were moist and her eyes… They were full of all kinds of mischief.

Then she took his hand and continued walking. Easy for her. He, on the other hand, had to do some discreet adjustments. Which didn't help. Thinking of baseball scores didn't, either.

Walking to the hotel had seemed like such a good idea.

MEG HAD TO WORK at not laughing. Not because she had teased Alex so unmercifully, but because she'd forgotten how this felt. She was on fire. Alive. And so turned on she could probably light up the whole island. They'd had banter. Actual banter. "Wow," she said.

Alex looked at her, a little confused. "The beach?"

She shook her head. "Us."

"Oh?"

"It's like when we're online," she said happily.

He slowed his step as he nodded. "Yeah, it is."

"That's very cool," she said.

"Very," he agreed.

She gave him a little hip bump. "Tell me what we're doing first."

"I thought we'd go to the activities desk and get our schedules," he suggested.

"Good thinking," she said.

"And what time is dinner?" he asked.

"Eight."

"Which means we have three hours to find interesting things to do with ourselves." He bumped her back with his hip. "We could always go back to the bungalow."

"Um…"

"Kidding. I'm kidding," he said.

"No, you're not," she countered.

"Hey, when I mentioned honesty, I didn't mean *that* honest," he protested.

Meg laughed, and bumped him once more. She liked this. She felt more relaxed now, with the cards on the table. They were going to have sex. Cool. Just not right now. "You mentioned drinks, yes?"

"I did. There's a bar. Actually, there are several bars, and they serve many wonderful tropical drinks," he told her.

"Mmm," she said, sounding a lot like Homer Simpson, "tropical drinks."

"Banana Cows. Tropical Jade. Between the Sheets. Parcha con China. And the ever popular Sex on the Beach," he said.

"Ooh, that sounds good."

He laughed, and the sound made her tingle in interesting places. "Which one?"

"The last five," she answered.

He pulled her close as a guy on a bike swooped past. She doubted she'd been in any real danger, but Alex's protectiveness was a delightful surprise.

His arm moved smoothly around her waist, and it was so nice, she did the same to him. They continued walking, passing some other vacationers, a few at first, then more. She couldn't remember seeing so many people smiling. Just smiling.

The hotel came into spectacular view, and it was more impressive than she'd remembered from earlier. "It's like a postcard."

"Especially with all those attractive people running around. Have you noticed?" he asked.

"It's hard not to. I wonder if they prescreen," she said.

"Or maybe everyone's not that attractive. Maybe they're just happy."

She squeezed him tighter. "You are such a romantic."

"Am not."

"Ha. You think I'm not on to you, buddy? I so have your number," she said.

He squeezed her right back. "You know what? You do. And that's just fine with me."

She let her head drop to his shoulder. It fit to perfection.

6

THE BAR WAS AS EXOTIC and cool as everything else about the resort. A thatched roof, wonderful gold-on-black designs on backlit panels, several small tables, and, of course, tall seats that offered a panoramic view of the ocean. Reggae music wafted from hidden speakers and there were two couples dancing between the tables.

It was crowded, but not overly so. In fact, they scored two seats at the far corner of the bar, where it was relatively dark.

The bartender, in his Escapades uniform, came to them immediately. He smiled as if he meant it, and said, "I'm Reggie and you two look like you could use a drink."

Alex turned to her, waiting, but she had no idea what she wanted. She had no idea what was in any of the drinks he'd told her about. Never much of a drinker, she mostly stuck to white wine, but that seemed too mundane for a night in paradise. "What do you recommend?" she asked.

Reggie studied her for a while, his large dark eyes moving from her face to her hands and back again. "For you, I think Sex on the Beach."

Meg grinned, wondering if that was his stock answer for all the women, or if she was broadcasting something more than her desire to enjoy the local color. "Sounds great."

"And for me?" Alex asked.

"Ah, for you, sir, a .357 Magnum."

Alex chuckled.

Reggie went to the far side of the bar and Meg took the opportunity to scope out the people around them. To Alex's right were a young couple, early twenties, who were very tan and all smiles. Their drinks were half-gone, the sunny umbrellas lying on the bar top, and his hand was on her thigh. Quite high up her thigh.

They were very attractive, and this time Meg didn't think it was just happiness that made them so. They looked as if they'd stepped out of an ad in *Vogue* magazine.

The guy caught her staring, but before she could turn away, he winked at her. It made her blush, but in a good way. The bar stools were close enough that there was really no way to ignore the company.

"Hey," the young man said, shaking a lock of his sun-bleached hair out of his eyes. "How you doing?

The question made both Alex and the other woman turn. Meg couldn't help but notice that the woman, also blond, had no reservations about checking Alex out.

"Great," Meg replied. "You look like you've been here for a while."

"Six days," he said. "It's been awesome."

"I'm Meg," she said. "This is Alex."

The guy leaned over and extended his hand to Alex. "Jeff." He nodded at his companion. "Rachel."

The men shook hands, and Meg figured that would be that, but their bar buddies shifted to more comfortable positions for conversation.

"When did you guys get here?" Rachel asked.

"Today. We're here for five days, and it looks like that's not going to be enough time to do everything. I can't believe how much is packed into this little island," Alex said.

"You've gotta check out the diving," Jeff said. "It's the best. Especially down by the cove. There's a coral reef there that's incredible."

"We're signed up to snorkel," Meg said. "What else have you done?"

"The rock wall was cool," Rachel said. "And we've been on the Jet Skis. Too much fun."

"Sounds like it," Alex reached over for Meg's hand and she felt instantly better, which was odd because she hadn't felt bad. She squeezed gently to let him know how welcome his touch was.

Reggie came over and put their drinks on coasters. "Enjoy."

Meg nodded her thanks, loving the look of the frosty tall glasses, and, of course, her very own tiny umbrella. She remembered their conversation on her birthday, still amazed that Alex had convinced her to come. Glad though. Because later…

She took a sip of the drink and found it icy and sweet, with hardly a hint of alcohol, although she was sure it was just masked by the juice. Since she was an admitted wuss when it came to the hard stuff, this suited her to a T.

"If you guys just got here today, then you haven't been to the disco, right?" Rachel asked.

Meg held her drink as she turned back to Rachel. "It's on the agenda."

"Great. We're going up later. And you do know that outside the disco, on the roof, there are Jacuzzis, right?" Rachel said.

"Nope, hadn't heard about those," Meg replied.

"Oh, yeah," Jeff said. "Sometimes it can get a little crowded, but it's worth it."

"I didn't bring my suit," Meg said.

Both Jeff and Rachel laughed.

"Oh," Meg said. "I had no idea. I thought there was just the nude beach on the other side of the cove."

"It's pretty loose. Although if you really want to get down, you go over to E.D.E.N.," Rachel said.

"What's that?" Meg asked.

Rachel grabbed her own drink, then leaned back against Jeff. His arm came around her waist and he rubbed small circles over her tummy. Rachel was wearing a bright, pink-hued sarong and Meg thought she looked amazingly sexy in it.

"E.D.E.N. is the sex camp," Rachel said.

"What?"

They both laughed again, but Meg's gaze had gone to Alex. He seemed as surprised as she was.

"We tried to get reservations there first," Rachel said, "but they were totally booked. It's supposed to be a real adventure, if you know what I mean. Orgasm classes, tantric sex, massage techniques. My sister and her boyfriend went a year ago, and it blew them away."

"I'll bet," Alex said. "I've never even heard of a sex camp."

"They don't advertise a lot." Jeff moved his hand up Rachel's stomach until his thumb brushed the underside of her breast. "They don't have to. There was a big article about the place in *Esquire,* though."

Meg's gaze was riveted by what was happening to Rachel. Jeff's ministrations were growing increasingly bold. His thumb had moved up her breast and the circles he traced were more powerful. Meg could see the pressure from here.

It made her own nipples tighten in sympathy, and she wished she could lean back against Alex. But she'd have to stand up, move the chair, and that would kind of spoil things.

Alex let go of her hand, but instead of getting his drink, he put his palm on her thigh. She looked at him and he smiled at her before his gaze shifted back to the Rachel and Jeff show.

When Meg looked up, her eyes met Rachel's.

"We've met some really cool people here," Rachel said, her voice a lot lower and smokier than just a moment before. "Open minded, you know? Adventurous."

Alex's hand squeezed her thigh, and that, combined with the images in Meg's head, made the heat rise from her throat to her face. She grasped the straw between her teeth and drank, picturing the four of them naked in the Jacuzzi. They were beautiful, and God knows Alex was sex on wheels. She'd never done anything remotely like a foursome, although she'd been invited once in college. Back then, the idea had frightened her into a stammering no, but it had fueled many a solo fantasy.

Now, here, when they were so far from anything resembling her normal life, she wasn't frightened in the least. The idea of hot sex with the three beautiful people in front of her intrigued her and made her terribly aware of the pressure between her legs, the tightness of her chest.

Intrigued, but that's all. She wasn't about to do anything with anyone except Alex. She wanted him, wanted his touch, his kiss. It seemed silly that she'd hesitated at all, although the idea of waiting appealed to her, too.

All she knew for sure was that Alex's hand had moved higher up her thigh, that his fingers had slipped to the tender flesh just below the crotch of her white panties, and she had to fight the urge to spread her legs, to throw back her head and let him do all manner of wicked things beneath the chaste covering.

Feeling his touch, his warm breath on her neck, she couldn't deny that she looked forward to the negotiations.

She closed her eyes and let her body slide down until his fingers touched the top of her inner thigh. Braver still, she parted her legs, not widely, but enough that he couldn't possibly mistake her move for anything but the invitation it was.

She heard a gasp, but when she looked up, she saw that no one was watching them at all. Rachel and Jeff were busy, the bartender was on the other side, and the gasp had come from Alex, followed quickly by the soft clunk of his glass being abandoned, and then the scrape of his bar stool. Shutting her eyes again, she felt his chest press against her as his arm circled her back. Then his fingers returned, his thumb rubbing against her moist panties.

She should have been much more embarrassed, knowing that the two strangers, not to mention the bartender and all the other patrons, only had to look at the right angle to be completely aware of what was going on. If she'd been this brazen at a bar in Los Angeles, she would have been asked to leave. But this wasn't L.A. It wasn't even the real world. Alex had taken her to an adult playground, one where the regular rules didn't apply.

She sighed, letting herself sink against his chest. She wished she hadn't been holding her drink, but she felt too wonderful to disrupt the flow by putting it down.

He continued to tease her with his lips. To kiss and nip and lick her temple and her cheek. She gasped as he slipped two fingers underneath the edge of her panties, touching her sensitized flesh for the first time.

He hummed in appreciation as he explored within the limited range. She could have made herself more available, but she didn't want to move an inch. The teasing was the sexiest thing she could remember, and when his other hand brushed the side of her breast, she squirmed. She had no choice.

"You're incredible," he whispered, his lips brushing the shell of her ear, his breath hot and tickling. "So soft. God, I want you."

She turned her head and met his gaze, and the fire she saw in his eyes was equal to her own. "I wish…"

"What?"

"No, never mind. This is perfect. For now," she whispered.

He grinned at her. "I knew you were a tease."

"If it was too easy, it wouldn't be fun," she said.

"Nothing about you is too easy. But damn, you're worth it."

"I'm glad you think so."

He leaned down and captured her lips in an awkward kiss, but it didn't matter. What she could get of him was enough.

Not for him, evidently, because the hand on her waist disappeared, his stool scraped, again and his head moved until his mouth could claim her fully.

He thrust his tongue into her mouth just as his finger slid between her lips to search and find her clit. He swallowed her sharp gasp as he rubbed her in tight, perfect circles.

She found his arm with her free hand and clutched her drink with the other. If he didn't stop, she was going to come, and while the prospect thrilled her, the knowledge that they weren't alone didn't. She pulled back. "Stop," she whispered.

Instantly, he obeyed.

She pushed his arm down gently and, quick on the uptake, he slid his hand from beneath her dress. He trailed his damp fingers down her thigh, and then rested his hand just above her knee.

Worried that she'd disappointed him, she turned to catch his eye. His smile quirked but his eyes were sympathetic, and for that she was very grateful.

He sat back on his stool, and she did the same, stealing a glance to her right, a little afraid to find an audience. Everyone seemed to be occupied by their own dramas. When she finally looked at Rachel and Jeff, she bit her lip to stop from laughing.

Clearly, Rachel didn't share Meg's inhibitions. She and Jeff were all over each other.

Alex chuckled, and she turned her attention to him. He leaned close. "You're blushing."

"I guess anything goes here, huh?"

His hand moved up her leg. "Anything. I want to give you every one of your fantasies, make every whim come true. Anything you want, Meg."

She shivered as his words traveled through her veins, through her blood, and pooled in the tight, hot wetness between her legs.

She'd been right all along not to speak to him on the phone. His voice was whiskey and velvet, stroking her as sensually as his nimble fingers.

This was what she'd been afraid of. This thrumming in her limbs, between her legs, awakening long dormant sensations, feelings she'd only dreamed of in secret.

Wanting this, wanting him, was dangerous. Having him was lunacy. Her life was so far from here, a million miles away. When he was words on a screen, she could pretend just enough. But the pretense had ended the moment he'd made her tremble. The emptiness of everything back home pressed against her. Five days of tasting heaven, and then back to…

"Meg?"

She looked at him, at the concern in his eyes.

"Are you all right?" he asked.

She nodded. "Take me somewhere else. I need to move."

He slipped the glass from her hand and put it on the bar top, then stood, held out his hand.

Behind him, Jeff and Rachel were snuggling, oblivious to anyone outside their circle of two.

It still excited Meg, what she and Alex had done, but she hadn't been prepared for the fear. She'd built a whole private world around Alex. It was the place she went when she was lonely or needed a shoulder to cry on. The man in her head was not the man holding her hand. He was real. Flesh and blood and sexy as sin.

God, enough with the doubts. She wanted him. And everything he'd promised.

7

ALEX STEERED MEG TOWARD THE hotel pool. He wasn't sure what she wanted to do, but for the moment, he wanted to walk on this almost empty path away from the bar so he could get himself calmed down. He knew she wasn't *trying* to kill him, but stopping him when he was as hard as he'd ever been was not good for his health. Something had to give, he just wasn't sure what. Maybe during dinner his head would explode.

He didn't even dare look at her. Not yet. Because, jeez. She'd felt amazing, and when her breath got all raspy and her eyelids fluttered, he nearly came without a single touch.

She seemed to be handling things pretty well. He remembered a late night session they'd had, one of the many where they discussed their fantasies. He'd asked her about doing it where they might get caught, and she'd been pretty interested. He'd asked her if she was a member of the mile high club, and she'd just laughed. He grinned. Online, her laughter was a series of HAHA-HAHAs, and he could tell how amused she was by how long it went on. Twice he'd earned a two-liner. That had pleased him inordinately.

Now that he knew the real sound, it would all be different. Sure, he'd still use the length litmus test, but now he'd hear her. By the time they went home, he wanted to hear every expression she had. Laughter, pleasure, satisfaction, and most especially he wanted to hear her come.

Bad thought. Okay, his seventh grade math teacher, Miss Cardinal. She'd been as ugly as a fireplug.

"Where are we going?" Meg asked, just as he shuddered.

"I thought we'd check out the rock wall. It's behind the pool. Then we can go inside and get our activities schedule." He squeezed her hand. "Sound okay?"

"Great. I think the sun sets in about an hour, yes? Maybe we can find a nice place to watch it. Another bar, perhaps?"

"You're smart and beautiful. Go figure," he teased.

She bumped into him, with her hip again. He liked that. Christ. It had been too long since he'd been on vacation. Especially with anyone like Meg.

"Alex?"

"Yeah?"

"How come you never told me about your family?" she asked.

"Where did that come from?"

"Don't know," she said. "It just occurred to me that I don't believe you've mentioned them at all."

"I haven't?"

"Nope. I've told you about mine," she said.

"You only had your mom and dad. I have siblings," he stated.

"Well?"

He sighed. "Okay, the *Reader's Digest* version. My parents live in Boston. He's a superior court judge, she's a criminal attorney for a huge firm. A partner. My brother, Lucas, is also an attorney, but he lives in New York. He's also a partner in his firm. My sister, Carra, is a pediatrician in Connecticut, married to another doctor, a neurologist, and they have two kids who are being raised by their Haitian maid."

"Pressure much?"

He laughed. "Ya think?"

"I know you got the grades. And you're one of the youngest columnists at the *Post*. So they must be happy, yes?"

"For the most part," he said.

"What more could they possibly want?" she asked.

"For me to be a real journalist. The kind with cover stories in *Time* and *Newsweek*. They want me to go to Europe, cover international politics. They want me to get a Pulitzer. At least that's the stated goal. What they secretly dream of is for all of us to get Nobel prizes, preferably in the same year, although the logistics of that are a bit fuzzy."

Meg shook her head. "That's nuts."

"Yep. My family. Overachievers of the first order. Nothing is good enough until it's better than everyone else on the planet."

"That must have made growing up a complete joy," she said.

"Oh, yeah. Although I'll give them credit. They loved their kids. We got the finest things money could buy. And not to turn out ungrateful or entitled, we all had to work. I started at fourteen with a paper route. I paid for my own apartment when I went to Harvard, and I bought my own first car," he said.

"That's not a bad thing," she stated.

"No, it isn't. I got a lot out of it. A good work ethic. A sense of responsibility. My passion for politics started when I worked for the Clinton campaign in '92. Before that, I was going to be an attorney," he said.

"Clinton, huh?"

"Basically, I worked for him just to piss my father off, but I fell in love. Not with Bill, but with the process. I summered in D.C. and that was it, I was hooked. It was the most exciting place I'd ever been. The power was so great, the machinations so Machiavellian, who could resist?"

"Why didn't you go into politics?" she asked.

He looked at her, surprised. "Be a politician? God, no. I never had any desire to run for office. I wanted to be the voice of honesty, a standard bearer for the people. Jeez, was I full of crap."

"What do you mean? Your column is exactly that. I think what you do is tremendously important."

"I'm a glorified gossip columnist," he said, his voice dripping with sarcasm. "There's nothing important about that."

She pulled him up short, and when he wouldn't face her, she walked around until she faced him. "Are you joking?"

"No. I'm desperately serious," he said.

"I'm confused. I read your column. Thousands of people read your column. Maybe hundreds of thousands, now that you're online. And you don't believe you have influence?"

"Oh, I have influence all right, but not the kind you mean. You think we can talk about something else?" he asked.

"No, we cannot. I want you to explain this."

"What about that no talking about work rule? Huh? That was your idea and it was very, very wise."

"I don't care. I need to understand," she insisted.

He thought about kissing her, but that wasn't fair. Then he thought about running, but that would reveal far more than he wanted her to know. Instead, he looked her straight in the eye. "Let me explain how my job works. People tell me secrets. Some are big and some are small, but they're like currency changing hands. Each secret begets power. It's easy to stockpile secrets, to use them, manipulate them. When you know people's secrets, they scurry like rats to find bigger secrets, more to trade.

"Most of them never hit the column. Sometimes they're hinted at, but never truly spilled, not if the secret is to remain currency. Once it's out in the open, the power disappears from the equation, and you're left with nothing to barter."

"So you're saying you hold all these Washington secrets, right?" she said.

"Not anymore," he stated.

"Excuse me?"

"It's a really long story. So I'll once again give you the *Reader's Digest* version. Before I left, I wrote three columns, the first one to run this morning. And in them, I cashed in. Spent all my secrets."

"I don't understand."

He wiped a hand over his face, knowing he had to tell her, but speaking the words aloud was making the whole thing awfully real. "For a long time now, what I knew was making me uncomfortable. I would look at my files and think about all I'd learned, all the crap I'd been told, bits at a time. And I was playing that crap as if I was playing chess. It was a big old game, and the American people weren't even on the board. The only players were the ones with the secrets. I didn't want to play anymore. So I told them. Everything I could, at least. I made sure I didn't reveal anyone's name I shouldn't. I didn't breach national security. But I've thrown a hell of a big stone into the pond, and the ripples are going to get everyone wet."

She stared at him in surprise. "I get the concept, but can you be a little more specific?"

"Okay. There's a congressional aide I know, name of Tracy Nolan. We had lunch about a month ago, and she let it slip that Congressman Kincaid has been spending several nights a week with an eighteen-year-old intern. Kincaid won in his district with lots of speeches proclaiming he would bring a new level of ethics to Washington, and was a strong proponent of banning gay marriage. Oh, did I mention the intern was male? And that Kincaid is married?

"When I spoke to Kincaid, he told me about Congressman Trask, who is also a member of the ethics committee. Trask, it turns out, has taken hundreds of thousands of dollars in contributions from a company that owns hundreds of Internet pornography sites. I cornered Trask, and he suggested my time might be better spent investigating another congressman who sits on a Pentagon procurement committee despite the fact that nearly five million dollars worth of stock in an armament company his committee recommended is in his wife's name."

Alex sighed. "What did I report on? The armament story. What should I have written about? All of it. Every last word of every last travesty. But I didn't. Until now."

"Are you going to be fired?"

"Not fired. Questioned, for sure. Retired, definitely. My usefulness to the paper is over..."

"But your editor. He had to have approved this, right?"

"He had no choice. We both know that without sources, there's no column."

"Well, damn," she said.

"That about sums it up," he agreed.

She nibbled her lower lip for a moment. "What happened?"

"What do you mean?"

"Something must have happened. You said your passion was politics. That you'd never been anywhere more exciting."

He smiled. "You."

She continued to stare, her big round eyes seeing something she hadn't been prepared for. That wasn't a guess, either. Disillusionment was his area of expertise. He could spot it a mile away.

"I know, it doesn't make a lot of sense on the surface, but when we talked, it was as if I'd found a part of me that I'd thought I'd lost. It made me think. About who

I'd become, and what I was doing with my life. I didn't like what I saw. So, I decided to do something about it," he said.

"How did I not know this?" she asked.

"Well, that's the only part I'm sorry about. And one of the reasons we're here. So I could tell you."

"But you said this change has been coming for a long time."

Alex nodded. "It has. For almost a year."

"Wow. I'm not sure how to feel about this. I mean, I believe what you did was a good thing, but where does it leave you?"

"Not where I was. I've been kicking a few ideas around about what I'm going to do. I haven't firmed up any decisions yet. But leaving D.C. is high on the list. A book, maybe. I don't know," he said.

"But…" She stared at him for a long time, her gaze intent and piercing. He let her look. Opened up as much as he knew how. It wasn't comfortable, but this was Meg, and she needed to understand.

"Okay," she said, finally.

"Okay?"

"I get it, although I'm still not sure how I fit into it all. Bottom line, I believe in you," she declared.

"You do?"

She nodded with such seriousness it made his throat clench.

"Telling the truth matters. Being who you're meant to be matters. I'm proud of you, Alex."

"Oh, God. Why did we wait so long to meet?" he said.

"Because we're both socially retarded."

He couldn't hold back another second. He had to kiss her. Moral imperative. So he did.

She kissed him back with such tenderness he wanted to carry her straight back to the bungalow, and never let her go.

He hugged her so tight she gasped. He relaxed his grip and pulled back from her lips. "We're in the most beautiful place I know of, with perfect weather, perfect views from everywhere, and we're going to find out all kinds of wicked things about each other. It doesn't get better than this."

She smiled at that.

"Am I right?" he asked.

"Yes. But—"

He put two fingers over her lips. "No buts. So no more talk of work, and this time, we stick to the deal."

"You're quite manipulative, did you know that?" she said.

"Yes, I did," he stated.

She frowned.

Damn, but she was stunning. "On the plus side, I'm very good at many naughty things," he teased.

She burst out laughing, cutting the tension, which had grown too thick.

"What in hell does that have to do with anything?"

He took her hand in his and tugged her along. "You'll see, my dear. You'll see."

8

THE FIRST THING THEY FOUND out when they got to the activities desk was that there was an opening for a couple's massage at the spa, but they had to hurry.

They crossed the lawn quickly, and went into the magnificent reception area. Someone different was behind the marble desk, but he smiled and welcomed them with the trademark grace of Escapades. After they filled out some very brief forms, mostly asking about trouble areas and allergies, he led them to separate locker rooms.

In his, Alex expected to smell the universal odor of locker room chlorine. Instead, it was something sweet and flowery, not in the least overdone. The towels were white and fluffy, and the sheet he was told to wrap around himself once he was naked felt great. He was also given a pair of slippers. New. Soft. Blue. They'd thought of everything.

Stripping off his pants, he realized there might be a downside to the couple's massage and it was sticking out from his groin at the three-quarter position. One look at Meg in her sheet, and he was sure to be saluting at full attention.

If they wanted to rub his chest, there was definitely going to be some tent action going on. Maybe he could ask that the masseuses wear blindfolds? Damn, he should have made up something on that form about how he was phobic about being rubbed on his chest.

Of course, this being Escapades, and these being massages for couples, well, they'd probably run across this situation before, right? Lots of times. Probably every guy who'd ever been on the table had risen to the occasion.

So he wouldn't be weird about it. They wouldn't even notice. With all this health stuff, they probably just figured it was a normal, human reaction. No big deal.

He headed out, holding the sheet out from the front of his body.

Meg was already there, draped like him. She was far more covered than she'd been in either her dress or her bathing suit, but see, he knew she was naked under there. That another woman was going to be rubbing delicious body parts with oils. Oh, shit.

"Alex? Is something wrong?"

"Uh, we have a minute or two, right? A couple, maybe five minutes?"

"I'm sure we do." She seemed confused. Which was better than her understanding his dilemma.

"Why don't you get settled, and I'll be back," he said quickly.

"Okay." She nodded, taking a step toward him.

He turned around, too fast, evidently, because his heel caught the sheet, and despite his hold, pulled it off.

Almost off. His ass was bared, but the sheet caught in front. On his now fully saluting dick.

Life was just so goddamn amusing.

MEG'S DRINK WAS SITTING on a little white table and the view from the tent was spectacular. The spa itself was situated on a rise so there was nothing but a few palm trees between her and the ocean and the sky.

The massage tables were set up just far enough apart that the therapists could fit between them. She'd be completely aware of what was happening to Alex, and he'd hear every moan and whimper from her.

She chuckled again, feeling badly for him. When the sheet had dropped, she'd deduced his predicament. It made her very glad that she didn't have a penis. Poor guy.

She'd also guessed his intention. For a moment, she'd thought about following him into the men's locker room and helping him solve the problem, but if there were other men in there, they might not understand that her motivations were completely unselfish. Besides, she wasn't even sure if Alex would be thrilled if she offered her services.

Anyway, she needed a few moments alone to digest what he had told her about his column.

Evidently, there'd been a lot more going on behind the scenes than she'd picked up on.

She just didn't understand why he hadn't said anything about this before. He'd told her so much about himself, and yet the really personal stuff, about his family, about his work struggles, he'd kept to himself.

Although, now that she thought about it, he'd given

her hints. Just a couple of weeks ago, he'd talked to her about reinventing himself. It had been a fascinating conversation, but she'd thought he'd been encouraging her to leave the mountain. Frankly, it hadn't occurred to her that he was the one seeking change. Which, she supposed, said more about her own problems than his. How many other talks had she misinterpreted? Was she the most selfish woman on earth, or what?

She picked up her Sex on the Beach and took a really big drink. The cold helped, but she thought the alcohol might help more. The longer she spent with Alex the more confused she grew. The only thing she was completely clear about was wanting him.

The swish of a curtain behind her made her turn, and there were the masseuses. One blonde, one dark, both wearing starched white uniforms and nurse's shoes, each with towels draped over forearms.

"Hi," the blonde said. "I'm Gwen and this is Neva." She looked around. "Your partner isn't coming?"

"He'll be out in a minute. We're both looking forward to this very much."

The women went over to cabinets set up on either side of the tent to plug in hot pots, which meant there would be warm oils, a fact that made Meg very happy.

"Would you like to look through our CD collection? If you'd like music, of course."

"Sure." She went over to Neva, who handed her a large CD case. Meg flipped through slowly, wondering just how long Alex was going to be. Most of the music was either classical or New Age. But toward the end she found something that made her smile. It was jazz, and it was damn good jazz. Something she knew Alex was fond of. Lionel Hampton. "Black and Blue." She pulled it out and gave it to Neva. Just then, Alex came back.

She had to look. The sheet fell in a nice, straight line down the front of his body. When she glanced up, he blushed. Poor baby. Gathering her own sheet, she put her drink down, went over and hugged him, hard.

"Uh, I appreciate the support, but this is a little counterproductive, if you know what I mean," he said.

Holding back a laugh, she let him go. "Let's do this, shall we?"

"We shall."

She went to the table on the right, Gwen's, and he went to Neva's. Meg opened her sheet and lay facedown on the table. It occurred to her that she'd have to look up every so often to see the sunset, which was growing more beautiful by the second.

She heard Alex get on his table, and then the music started.

"Hey."

She turned her head to face him. "Surprise."

"Did you arrange this?"

"It would have been much cooler if I had, but no. It was among the CDs."

"Excellent choice."

She put her head down on the crescent headrest and sighed, letting her thoughts be carried away by the breeze. The music eased her passage into a state of near ecstasy, and with the first touch of Gwen's hand, she whimpered, which was kind of odd since all Gwen did was put her hair into a towel.

When the actual massage began, Meg went into the zone. But it was a different zone than she'd ever experienced before. Because this time, Alex was there.

Her eyes were closed, her head was down, and yet all she truly wanted to do was think about the hours they'd spent together. She couldn't recall a time that she'd enjoyed more. His humor was even better in person. Funny what you missed without the inflections, the facial expressions. He was incredibly adorable in every way that mattered.

It was hard not to think about leaving him, but when she did, she clamped down tight, refusing to entertain those pesky thoughts. She had him now. Had him right there, moaning next to her.

She grinned. Clearly, Alex was enjoying himself. So he was noisy. Well, that was good, because she was, too. It had gotten her into trouble, so she tried to contain herself, but dammit, it was just one of those things.

Besides, if all went well, there was no way she was going to be quiet with him. God, how she wanted him. So much it was a physical ache, not something Gwen could rub out or soothe. Only one thing could ease her, and that was Alex.

It gave Meg an extra thrill to know that he'd had to take care of himself because of her. She actually felt proud. As if she'd done something extraordinary. Oh, tonight was going to be one for the books.

"A little tense here, yes?"

Gwen was working on her shoulders, and Meg figured she'd better stop thinking about Alex or this massage wasn't going to have the desired effect. The more Gwen rubbed, the easier it was to sink into pure, unadulterated heaven.

IT HAD TAKEN ABOUT ten seconds and the merest touch to take care of his little problem. But it had taken him considerably longer to regain his air of cool machismo and walk out of the men's room. He'd thought he'd gotten his act together pretty well until Meg, wrapped in her towel, her beautiful shoulders so tantalizing he wanted to lick them all over, had hugged him.

He'd accepted that he wasn't a kid any longer, and he'd also accepted what that meant. Downtime wasn't a luxury, it was a necessity. And yet her body pressed against his and bingo, a twitch and more.

So among the other things that Meg could do so effortlessly was turn back the clock. Who knew?

Maybe it was the anticipation. The idea that tonight he'd have her all to himself, to do many wicked and wonderful things. Knowing her secrets was more of an aphrodisiac than he'd have ever guessed. What he had to do now, however, was not think about them. Not even the one where she wanted to be tied up—

Miss Cardinal. Miss Cardinal.

Okay, that was better. It didn't help that the masseuse was turning his muscles into passive, obedient noodles. He moaned. It was so damn good. She knew exactly where to put the pressure, and she took no prisoners. Yeah, it hurt, but it hurt just right.

She moved her strong hands down his back, working slowly, carefully and with such dedication he wanted to give her a medal. It was a gift, and if he could afford it, he'd fly to the island weekly, just for this.

Maybe he could arrange things so the masseuse would come to the bungalow. Oh, man, the thought of just rolling from the table to the bed was the thing dreams were made of.

No, wait. Him being a limp noodle when he was in bed with Meg wasn't quite what he'd pictured.

The masseuse hit a particularly sore spot at the lower end of his back and he grunted. She eased up. "No, it's okay," he said.

The pressure came back, and along with it came the ache. Why did some pain feel so good? Maybe because of the knowledge that it was healing pain?

Ah, who the hell cared.

This was exactly what he needed. Not just the island, but the woman. Meg, not the masseuse. She was something else. He wished she could see how the job was eating away at her. It was incredibly obvious. In an odd twist of fate, it was watching Meg's struggle with her image of herself that had helped him see himself for the first time in years.

Meg felt she owed it to her father, but dammit, from what she'd told him, her father wouldn't have wanted that from her. Not everything. He'd been a good man. Surely he'd want his child to have some fun, to fall in love, to get married. But that wasn't going to happen as long as she was wed to the people on that mountain.

Alex would find a way to talk about it, so that it wouldn't threaten her. No one else was stepping up to the plate. He knew Meg had friends, but she rarely had time to see them. She'd turned to him when she needed to vent, and he'd paid attention.

A major part of setting up this trip had been to get her alone, so she couldn't sign off from the computer when things got too uncomfortable. He wasn't going to let it go, not when she needed so badly to see what she had given up, continued to give up, in the name of misguided loyalty. If he could cast off his shackles, so could she.

But that was for later. The only talk they were going to have, once they got to the bungalow, was going to be said in between gasps and orgasms.

He focused on the music, on those sultry sounds that were such a part of his world. He felt the warm oil on the warm hands as they kneaded his flesh. Mostly, he thought about what a lucky son of a bitch he was, and that he wanted to remember everything. He'd need these memories when he was back in D.C. He had a lot of people to face, a lot of decisions to make. It would make things easier if he could slip into thoughts of Meg.

"Sir?"

He heard the whisper, and grunted to let her know he was awake.

"Why don't we take a small break. The sunset is so beautiful, I'd hate for you and your lady to miss it."

"A break?"

"Don't worry," she said, in her lilting Jamaican accent. "I'm going to help you sit up, and while you're sipping your delicious drink, I'm going to work on your feet."

"My feet?"

She leaned down a little lower. "You're going to love it."

He believed her.

Her arm, quite strong, reached beneath his shoulder until he could gather the sheet and sit up. He turned his head to find Meg, already seated, a big wedge thing behind her back.

His wedge came as soon as he was settled, and it was remarkably comfortable. Then the two women brought low stools and sat down in front of them, out of his sight.

Meg grinned at him as if they'd won the lottery, and she held up her drink, umbrella and all. A slight lean to the left and he had his own drink. He raised it to her.

A few sips later, his right foot was caressed, and there was warming oil and the most incredible touch. He sighed, looking out at the fire-bright sky. Purple, pink, orange, all mixed together with exquisite care. Without even looking, he reached out his free hand, and there it was: Meg's hand, reaching right back.

9

MEG FOLLOWED THE HOST out to the restaurant patio, consumed with the feeling of Alex's hand on the small of her back.

It was full-on night now, and a gorgeous one at that, but the patio was illuminated with torches, lots of them, which made everything shimmer. They were seated with an unobstructed view of the beach. Their table was far enough from the others that they could talk easily. Music wafted over the deck—nothing too intrusive, kind of soft and tropical.

Meg picked up the menu. It was huge, and the first three pages were all drinks. Fabulous-sounding drinks made with fruit and rum, and she wanted to try them all. But since she'd already had two, she figured she'd better cool her jets. It was still fun to read the descriptions. "Hey, Alex, here's one you should try. Sweet Death Becomes Her."

"Her?"

"I don't think it actually turns you into a girl."

"Phew. And it would be…?"

"Malibu rum, silver rum, 151 rum, spiced rum and pineapple juice."

"You know you can have your way with me without making me too drunk to protest."

"You're easy. I get it."

He laughed. "I'm going to stick with the Magnum. Don't want to mix my juices. What about you?"

"Iced tea. The regular kind, not Long Island."

"Chicken."

"I'd like to stay awake until we're back at the bungalow."

"Good thinking." He went back to the menu, but she could see his eyes were crinkled from his smile.

She turned to the food portion, but she had the same problem there as with the drinks. It all sounded incredible, and although it felt as if she could eat all of page six, she knew she really couldn't. The simplest way around this was to order the special fish of the day, whatever it was.

When she looked up again, the waiter, dressed in the blue-and-white tropical shirt that all the staff wore, was standing at the ready.

"Will there be cocktails to begin?"

Meg was just about to order when the hostess led a couple to the table next to theirs. Not just any couple—Walter and Tina.

Meg thought of diving underneath the table, but there was no time, and besides, they'd notice. Instead, when Tina said, "Hi!" with such obvious pleasure, Meg smiled. It wasn't the end of the world, or even the end of the evening. She and Walter were probably very sweet people.

"Well, isn't this a happy coincidence," Tina said, as they approached the table.

"Yes, it is," Meg replied, not daring to look at Alex. Of course she wanted their dinner to be private, but there was no way she was going to be rude. They'd just have to keep their voices down, that's all.

The hostess smiled brightly, holding the large menus against her blue floral shirt. "You know each other? How nice. Would you like to sit together?"

Now Meg shot a panicked glance at Alex. His eyes were wide, blinking, and she knew he was searching frantically for a reason to say no, just as she was. But a brilliant response wasn't forthcoming, not before Tina said, "That's a wonderful idea, if we're not intruding."

"No, of course not," Meg said. She pointed to the two free chairs. "There's plenty of room."

She felt Alex kick her under the table, but she didn't even wince. The truth was, she'd heard the desperation in Tina's voice, and she couldn't ignore it.

It took a few minutes for them to get settled, with Brian, their waiter, hovering. Walter ordered drinks for himself and Tina. Alex asked for a .357 Magnum, and even though Meg really wanted a stronger drink, she went for the iced tea.

They all needed to read the menus, and that took a few minutes. She kept glancing over at Alex, who had a smile pasted on his face that barely disguised the annoyance in his eyes. Her tummy tightened with worry. Who would Alex be in a situation like this?

Brian came back with their cocktails, and then everyone ordered. Walter eschewed the local fare for a steak, which Meg didn't understand. When in Rome… She ordered the catch of the day, and Alex chose some shrimp concoction. Tina got into the spirit and decided on jerk chicken.

After the waiter left, Meg lifted her drink and held it up, catching Alex's gaze. "To adventures," she said.

For the first time since Walter and Tina had joined them, his smile reached his eyes. "To adventures," he echoed.

They toasted, and their company joined in. After a long sip, Meg turned to Tina, figuring she was the one who needed to talk. "How did you two end up here?" she asked.

"Our children surprised us for our anniversary. Twenty-five years." Tina shook her head. "It seems impossible, but there you have it."

"Congratulations."

"Thank you. It's our first vacation in…" She glanced at Walter, who looked as if he'd rather be anywhere other than Escapades. "I don't remember. A long time. Walter owns a printing plant and business has been booming. We don't seem to have much time off."

"We had no business leaving now, either. Martin's making a complete mess out of the history text, and who's going to pay for that, eh? It's not coming out of his paycheck."

"That was very nice of your kids," Meg said, not sure it was all that polite to ignore Walter's comments, but more concerned with Tina than him.

"It was." Tina reached over to meet Walter's hand on the table, but he didn't notice. She drew back, a slight blush pinking her cheek. "They're good kids. Danny's a pharmacist. He's engaged to a wonderful girl. And Elizabeth is studying English literature at Northwestern." She brightened a bit after taking a sip of her drink. "What about you two?"

Alex chuckled. "Yeah, what about us two?"

"We've been online friends for a long time. This is our first real date," Meg explained.

"My goodness," Tina said. "Walter, did you hear that?"

Walter looked up. "Never met before, huh?"

"Nope," Alex said. "First time."

Walter pulled his cell out of his pocket and put it on the table, right next to his salad fork.

"That seems very brave," Tina said. "I'll admit, I don't know much about online dating, but I hear it's very popular."

"It's working out pretty well." Meg waggled her brows at Alex. "Of course, this is just day one. We'll see how we feel after four more days."

Alex coughed, and then she felt his foot touch hers again. He lifted his drink in such a way that only she could see his lips. He mouthed, "This sucks."

She laughed, then coughed to cover it up. Not trusting herself to even look at him, she turned back to Tina. "Where are you from?"

"Iowa. Walter's plant is the largest in the state. He does the printing for two big magazines, but mostly, he prints textbooks."

"Do you work at the plant?"

Tina shook her head. "No, I was a stay-at-home mom. Which was wonderful when I had children to stay home for." She looked at Walter again. His gaze was on his phone, though, and Meg wondered if he knew how unhappy his wife was.

"So now it's time to find something new," Meg said. "What do you love to do?"

Tina laughed. "Love to do? Good grief. Well, I read a lot. It's about the only thing I'm good at. I tried knitting and I'd rather stick the needles in my eyes. I've managed to kill every plant I've ever owned. So it's back to books."

"Books are wonderful. You know, Alex is a writer. He's a columnist for the *Washington Post*."

Finally, Walter perked up. "You write for the *Post*? What's your name?"

Meg grinned. "Alex Rosten."

Walter nodded and his lips actually curved a bit. "I've seen you on that morning news show on CNN."

Alex was spared a humble response when the food arrived, but the ice had been broken. For a little while, they all concentrated on their meals, but when Tina did try to include Walter, he either grumbled or ignored her completely. It wasn't fun sitting there, and Meg felt Tina's embarrassment acutely. The worst of it was when the cell phone rang, and Walter walked away without a word or a backward glance.

The whole encounter reminded her a little too much of what it had been like when she was growing up. It didn't matter what her family was doing—eating dinner, celebrating a birthday, if the phone rang, her father tuned them out as if they'd been a mildly interesting television show. Meg remembered a few times when her mother had objected, but it had been useless. The work came first and last.

With some guilt, she thought about the times she'd

left her friends in the lurch. No wonder her invitations had become so scarce. She'd fallen into the patterns she was raised with, and hadn't done a thing to find the kind of balance that could have made her family life one filled more with joy than tension.

The food was spectacular, and Meg focused on that instead of thoughts of Tina and Walter, which meant she ate far too much. She didn't even have room for dessert. She liked Tina, and wished things could be different for her. Maybe the island would work its magic on Walter. Stranger things had happened.

At last Tina folded her napkin on her plate, and touched Meg's hand. "Thank you for letting us intrude. It was a very nice dinner."

"I'm glad you were here," Meg said. "We'll see you back at the bungalows, I'm sure."

The older couple rose, and Walter shook Alex's hand before they left.

Meg watched them walk away. The second they were out of range, Walter got back on the phone. Tina's shoulders slumped as she walked slightly behind her husband. All Meg could do was think about what she'd done to herself, to her own life. Her work had become all-consuming. And in the end, what did it leave her with? What would she have when she was too tired to make the house calls? Memories of operations? Of birthing foals? Stitching up dogs? Could that possibly be enough?

ONCE THEY'D LEFT the restaurant and were on the path again, Alex pulled her into his arms. He looked at her, his eyes serious and his body warm. He didn't speak.

Instead, he kissed her. A long, slow, deep kiss that let her know he was glad they were alone again.

She was, too. Very glad, although she couldn't feel too bad about sharing dinner. But this—this was what she wanted. Alex. Just Alex.

Finally, he pulled back. She laid her head on his chest as he continued to hold her tight.

"Next time we go to dinner," he said, "let's make sure our table is just for two."

She nodded.

"For the record, I think you're an amazing person."

She looked up at him. "Really."

He smiled at her. "It might be a problem, you know."

"What?"

"You being so nice, and me, well… The first word that comes to mind is *asshole*. I'm sure there are more, but asshole pretty much sums it up."

"I don't believe that. Not for a second. You've been nothing but wonderful."

"You bring it out in me."

She thought about that for a moment. "You bring out good things in me, too. I guess that's why I couldn't wait to turn on the computer at night. It was the best part of any day."

He kissed her again, briefly, sweetly. "You want to go check out the disco?"

She shook her head. "Nope."

"Oh?"

"I forgot something at the bungalow," she said.

"You did? What?" he asked.

"To make love to you."

"Oh."

She took his hand in hers and turned toward the path to their end of the beach. "Any objections?"

"Not a one."

"Cool."

They walked, not rushing, content to be alone under the brilliant moon, letting the scented air slide over their skin. There were lots of people on the path now, some in bathing suits, some dressed to party. Almost all of them were touching, kissing. It was impossible to feel anything but romantic, but Meg knew her feelings had more to do with the man then the setting.

"You know," he said, "when I left D.C. it was snowing. I was afraid they might cancel the flight. I was flying to the tropics, but I needed to take my heavy coat because it was freezing out there. From the moment I got to the airport, I felt like I was cheating. Like I had something over all the poor schmucks going on their business flights, with their computers and Palm Pilots and cell phones attached to their ears. Despite the earthquake I was leaving behind, I was on vacation. But better than that, I was on vacation with you. We weren't going to meet for hours, but it didn't matter. You were already there. In my head. You have been for a very long time."

"Oh, my." She squeezed his hand as she thought about what lay ahead. She was going to have sex. With someone she liked so much. On an island. In February.

The last time she'd had sex had been, what, two years ago? And it hadn't been the stuff of dreams. He was just a guy she'd met at a seminar. Another vet. Which turned out to be a plus when, in the middle of the rather lack-luster boink, she'd had to leave. A sick dog. The guy had never called, and she hadn't cared.

"Hey, what's wrong?"

"Nothing." She pushed her hair behind her shoulder and tried to get back to being happy she was here with Alex.

"Come on. Something went south."

Searching for a dismissive lie, she couldn't think of a thing, until she remembered that this was different. She could tell him anything, right? "Just reliving my last date. If you want to call it that."

His steps slowed. "That bad, huh?"

She shrugged. "It wasn't awful so much as it was nothing. The heavens most definitely didn't part."

"Have they ever?" he asked.

"Maybe not the heavens. But I thought I was in love once," she admitted.

"You never mentioned that before."

"It wasn't a big deal. A college romance. Hank was a year older, and we were both studying our tails off. He ended up at a big animal hospital in Chicago, and that was it."

"He didn't break your heart?"

"Not really. I think the idea of him was more attractive than the man. And since then, it's been all work, all the time," she said.

"You're satisfied with that?" Alex asked.

"No. I want more. I just have to figure out how I'm going to get it."

"Move," he said.

"What?"

"Quit," he said. "Move. I know you love being a vet, but you can do that lots of places, in a practice that doesn't ask for your whole life."

"It's not that simple," she said.

"Why not?"

"I have obligations. My parents gave up everything for our practice. People count on me. I can't just walk away."

He nodded. "Okay, I get that. I understand all about obligations. But loyalties can be misplaced. It's not unheard of."

"Our situations are very different, Alex."

"All I'm saying is that work isn't everything," he insisted.

"No? So tell me about all the other rich things in your life. Pottery, perhaps? Maybe adult education classes?" she said, with a bite that surprised her.

"All right, so I don't have much of a life, but I'm not obsessive or anything."

"Ha."

"What about my novel?" he said.

"What novel?"

"The one I'm writing."

She stopped walking, pulling him up short. "You're writing a novel?"

"Yeah. I told you," he said.

"Alex, you did no such thing."

"I didn't?"

"No. You've never said a word about a novel. For heaven's sake. You didn't tell me you were thinking of relocating, you didn't tell me you'd decided to turn your life upside down hours before we met. Now this. Who are you?"

"You know me," he stated.

"No, clearly I don't."

"But you do. I tell you everything that matters," he said.

"Excuse me? Novel? Quitting? Huge work confessions? Those matter, Alex," Meg declared.

"Okay, I see your point. But I only get you for a few hours a week, and dammit, I don't want to waste it on that crap," he exclaimed.

Meg pushed her hair back. "Explain that to me please, because I don't get it at all."

"You're my dessert."

"Is that it? I'm a trifle?"

"God, no. I didn't mean it that way. Honestly."

"Hmm."

"Seriously. Come on, Meg. Please, please don't misunderstand me. I'm sorry."

"I don't want apologies, I want to understand. I tell you everything. I thought you told *me* everything."

Alex pulled her closer to him. "I do. But a lot of it is in my head."

"Hard for me to offer an opinion that way," she said.

"Oh, no. You do. All the time," he told her.

"Pardon?"

"You talk to me. In fact, you're the only one who'll tell me the truth. You could, by the way, be a little more tactful," he said.

"So, you're insane, and I'm the voice in your head?"

"Pretty much," he agreed.

Meg looked up at the moon. This was very confusing. And somewhat flattering. But mostly confusing. "Let's put the voices in your head aside for the moment, and get back to the novel." She looked at him once more.

"It's about Washington," he said.

"So far, so good."

"It's a thriller, and it's about politics," he continued.

"Well, that's great. It's certainly what you know," she said.

"But this is fiction."

"Didn't you used to write fiction?" she asked.

"That was in school. Hundreds of years ago. Millions," he said, sighing.

"When do you write?"

"Whenever I can. Every spare minute," he confessed.

"Which means you don't hate it. In fact, I believe that means you're enjoying the writing a lot," she murmured.

"It's hard. It's frustrating."

"Which makes it even better, right?"

His smile changed into one that made her want to kiss him. "Enough with the writing for now. You know all the important things about me, Meg."

"Setting off that grenade at work—so that's your way out?" she asked.

"That's part of it. Not the most important part."

"What is?"

"What matters is that I'm trying to get back to the me that was lost," he said.

They walked for a while in silence, Meg thinking about all the changes he was going through, and how hard it must be for him.

"You think we can use the phone now?" he suddenly asked. "I mean, when we go home?"

"Give up the computer?" she said.

"Nobody said we had to give it up. Can't we do both?"

"Do you think it'll be the same?" she wondered.

"No," he said. "I think it'll be better."

She didn't feel quite so sure.

"You don't want to talk to me when we get back?" he asked.

"Sure I do."

"Meg?"

"You do know how scary it was for me to come here. To see you. I love having you on the computer. You've been my safety net, my confidant," she said.

"Yeah. We're good when we're typing, aren't we?"

"And we're good here," she said, meaning it. "But this is Disneyland for grown-ups. This is tropical breezes and incredible sunsets and naughty touching in front of strangers."

"Ah, yeah. The good life," he joked.

She laughed. "Stop it. You know what I mean."

He nodded. "And I don't have a clue what my life is going to be like when we get back."

"Isn't it nice, then, to know exactly what we're going to be doing when we get to the bungalow?"

He smiled. "Oh, yeah."

10

THE FARTHER THEY GOT FROM the hotel, the more anx-
ious Alex became. Since the moment he'd seen Meg
standing at the airport, he'd wanted her. No, that
wasn't true. He'd wanted her before that. They'd had a
connection for almost a year, and not just the one over
the computer. Somehow, not meeting her in person had
freed something in him, allowed him to be more honest with Meg than with anyone else in his life.

That she was so beautiful was a bonus, but it wasn't
the reason. Meg had pulled him in subtly, with wise
words, candid conversation and a wry perspective that
made him think and laugh. A total surprise, given his
luck with women.

Not that he hadn't had his fair share, but even when
he'd thought he'd been in love, it had been a reasoned
decision. He wasn't in the least reasonable when he was
near Meg, and his ability to make decisions was somewhere at the caveman level.

"It's so beautiful out here," she said, leaning her head
against his shoulder. She'd taken off her shoes as they'd
veered from the path to walk in the sand.

His arm rested on the curve of her hip. When he felt

the urge, he drew her tighter, because it felt so good to have her body so close. But then he relaxed again. She wasn't going anywhere.

"Look."

He followed her gaze up to the sky and was surprised to see how huge the moon was. Just shy of full, it was brilliant in the darkness. He could see the shadows and crevices, the facelike craters that looked quite different when he was at his apartment in Alexandria. "It seems so near."

"Magic," she whispered.

"Definitely."

They kept walking, and he pondered taking off his shoes so he could join her in enjoying the warm sand between his toes, but he didn't want to stop. His entire body felt sensitized to every brush of the warm breeze. Every step felt sure and strong, and as his hand followed the curve from her waist to her hip, he found it hard to grasp that this was real.

Maybe it was the fact that he was in a new time zone, or that he'd had a few drinks, but he doubted it. Meg was right, it was magic, but it was magic because of her.

"Where are you?" she asked.

"Hmm?"

"You're here, but you're not. What's going on?"

He slowed his steps, then turned toward her. "It feels like this is a dream."

She nodded, but didn't speak. Her eyes reflected the moonlight, as did the hint of her white teeth between slightly parted lips.

"I don't want to get all, you know…" he said.

"What?"

"Mushy." He pushed out the word.

"Heaven forbid," she teased.

"Hey. You want to hear this?" he asked.

"Sorry. I'll be quiet. Go on."

He rolled his eyes. "Yeah, sure, now that my rhythm is all shot to hell."

"Don't make me pinch you," she threatened with a giggle.

"Fine, fine. Jeez. I can't believe you're really here. Okay? And that you're so damn incredible."

She took a deep breath, held it for a few seconds, then let it out slowly. "Oh, my."

"I know so much about you, yet there's so much I don't know. Today's been a revelation," he said.

"You're not disappointed?"

He shook his head. "You're beyond my wildest expectations."

"I see," she said. Then she turned back to face the ocean, and they continued walking.

A stab of hurt hit him low and hard, but he didn't say anything. He figured she must be absorbing his words, or maybe she was overwhelmed and didn't know how to respond. He couldn't let himself think it was because she didn't feel something. The way she'd kissed him, laughed with him, talked to him… No, he just had to be patient. No reason to regret telling her the truth, no matter what happened.

The sound of waves lapping at the shore grew louder as they walked in silence. Her grip on his hand firmed the closer they got to the water. Then Meg released him and stepped forward until her toes made impressions in the wet sand. She looked back at him, smiled but still, she didn't speak.

He crossed his arms over his chest, watching as the wind played with her hair, shifting it on her shoulders, on her bare upper back. His gaze moved down her slim silhouette, her dress conforming so well to her body.

She took careful, slow steps into the ocean. He couldn't look anywhere but where the water touched her flesh. As she walked, it rose past her ankles to her calves, until it rippled around her knees.

His respiration had increased as she entered the surf, as if he was touching her. A movement caught his eye, and he looked up to where her dress ended and her bare back began.

She'd brought her right hand around to the top of the zipper, and as he watched, she slowly, achingly, lowered the tab until the material parted, giving him a stunning view of the length of her spine. A glimpse of her shoulder blade made him gasp.

Once more she turned to glance back at him. Once more she smiled and said nothing.

When she faced the sea again, she let go of the zipper. Her dress gaped open, and his hand moved down to his own zipper. Rather, to what was beneath the zipper, as his arousal became so intense it was on the edge of pain.

Unblinking, he stared, completely unable to move.

Meg threw her head back as if she were about to laugh at the moon. Then she shook her lush behind, spread her arms, and the dress, the beautiful dress, slipped down her body until it floated around her knees.

Alex tried to look up, but for a long moment, all he could do was focus on the way the garment bobbed and pooled. It was like some strange sea creature, sparkling, undulating, touching her like a lover.

His gaze inched up her thighs, to the curve of her ass. And then he saw them. White panties.

He groaned, doubling over at the sight of this woman and what she'd done for him. It wasn't an actual fetish, but it was a definite preference that he'd mentioned once. Okay, twice. And she'd remembered.

Or maybe she always wore white panties.

He preferred the former idea. That she'd have thought about him, about their talks. He flashed on other things he'd said to her—things that perhaps she'd remembered, that she'd want to do. But he kept staring at her panties, even as she stepped out of her dress and walked farther into the deep.

The moment the water hit the tops of her thighs changed everything. It wasn't that he couldn't breathe, because he'd forgotten how when the dress had dropped. And it wasn't that he wanted her so intensely he could hardly stand it.

He needed her.

Needed to touch her, to please her, to give her everything she'd ever wanted. He needed to make her laugh, and to help her stop her insane work schedule. He needed the connection between them in every way possible. Online, on the phone, but mostly in the flesh. Preferably in bed, but he'd take what he could get.

This was not part of the agenda. In fact, it wasn't even in the realm of the possible.

What was real was that he had to get into the water.

He stripped his shirt off while he toed off his shoes. His pants were next, and he hissed as he cleared the zipper. He'd never undressed faster. He was glad she was still facing away when he headed out to meet her, because he was bob-bob-bobbing along.

The temperature of the water took care of that problem. Jesus. He'd expected the sea to feel warmer at night, and it was, well, not cold, but it wasn't warm. It actually wasn't bad once he got up to his thighs.

She was wet to her waist when she turned to face him. And she was laughing. "Finally."

"Huh?" he asked smoothly.

"It took you long enough to get the hint."

"Sorry. When the dress came off all the blood rushed from my brain."

She swished her hands in the water, making her breasts, which were stunning, jiggle. "Funny thing. There was only one acceptable excuse and that was it."

"Phew."

"It's marvelous, isn't it?" she said, sighing.

"Yeah."

"I meant the ocean. The island," she added.

"I meant you," he said quietly.

She stopped swishing and moved closer to him. So close, her breasts touched his chest. Her hips touched his. He couldn't take it one more second, and he grasped hold of her arms and pulled her to his mouth.

She tasted of the sea, and the heat of her warmed him all the way through.

She clutched his ribs and kissed him back. Kissed

him like she meant it. Tongues and lips and nipping teeth, and nothing held back. What a fool he'd been, hurt because she hadn't said the words. This proof was in the pudding.

When she pulled away, he moaned, and again she laughed, but he was catching on. "Your dress is probably floating to Tahiti, you know"

"Such a great loss," she said dryly, then paused for a moment. "I want…"

He swallowed. "What?"

"Everything."

He opened his mouth, but no words came as she brought her hands up to her breasts. She brushed her hard nipples with her palms and teased them with her fingertips.

Alex released his breath as his gaze moved from her chest to her face. Her eyes, caught in moonlight, were the sexiest thing he'd ever seen. Except for her tiny little grin, so full of mischief and promise.

He sucked in another breath, tasting the ocean. He'd rather taste her.

All it took was one step and she was in his arms, and his mouth was on hers, and there was nothing tentative or wary. She opened to him and he took advantage, plunging his tongue inside the wet heat. Her breasts pressed against his chest. As they moved, the water between them caused a friction that made him groan. He could feel her nipples, hard, beading, and he wished he had some of those new lotions that facilitated sex in the water.

The thought vanished as her tongue touched his. Goddamn, she tasted good. He pulled back, but only so he could change the angle, and her small whimper did something to his insides.

She moved her pelvis against him, with her lips open and her breath mingling with his own, the rubbing of her breasts making him insane. He couldn't wait another minute.

He kissed her again, hard, thrusting, letting her feel his intentions. She responded with a shift of her hips and her fingers tightening on his neck.

He pulled back, just enough. "Bed."

She nodded, swallowing thickly. "Bed."

He tugged her hands from behind his neck, holding on to her left one as he led her out of the water. He glanced back and lost his footing when he saw that the white panties had become transparent.

"Whoa, you okay?"

"Just hormonally challenged," he said as he straightened. "I'll be fine in six days."

She laughed, then continued to torment him by taking great big steps, which made things move in wonderful ways.

He turned away, not nearly coordinated enough to watch and walk at the same time. When they got to his clothes, he gathered them up quickly, then took a look along the shoreline to see if her dress had washed up. Nothing. When he turned back, Meg was taking off her white panties.

11

MEG WAS BREATHLESS WHEN THEY got to the bungalow, and it wasn't just because they'd practically run back. All her senses were on full tactical alert, ready for action and raring to go. Just looking at Alex made her want to throw herself on the bed and yell, "Take me, big boy, take me hard."

She laughed, and he laughed, too, although she was pretty damn sure she hadn't said that last bit aloud.

The moment didn't last. Before she could even catch her breath he had her up against the wall with his body flush against her own. One searing look and then a bruising kiss…

She opened to him, wanting him to take it all. Knowing he would. He rubbed his erection up against her, and it burned across her cold skin.

Her hands went to his back and she raked her nails over his shoulder blades. He growled low in his throat. That sound alone made her stomach clench with desire.

This was new, all new. Never before, not with any guy, had she felt this desperation. It truly felt as though if she didn't have him she would die.

He pulled away from her. She whimpered at the loss,

but then he grabbed her hand and dragged her toward the bathroom.

"Shower," he said.

She nodded. He dumped his clothes on the floor, turned on the light and the water, bending to check the temperature.

Meg took the opportunity to check out his body. Of course, she looked at his ass first, because, well, there it was. She'd been right when she'd seen him in his jeans. He didn't have one of those flat butts. His was round and nice, and she couldn't resist touching.

He stood straight with a gasp, making her laugh. Then he turned his head to look back at her, just as she'd done in the sea. "Impatient, are we?"

"We are."

He turned the whole way, and while she wished she had the good manners to look him in the face, she didn't. She looked down to the very respectable erection he sported. A clue that his impatience was just as fervent as her own.

She dipped her gaze just enough to see his thighs. Tension made the muscles bulge a bit. He shifted his stance, then, very slowly, brought his right hand up to skim the underside of his cock.

Her breath left in a whoosh and she felt all kinds of interesting things happen to the good parts of her body.

"It's hot," he said.

"I'll say."

Alex laughed. "The water."

Her head went up with a snap. "Ah."

He moved aside, letting her get near the shower stall.

She stuck her hand in to make sure it wasn't too hot, then stepped in under the spray. The pressure was perfect, and the showerhead was high enough and long enough that it made her think it had been designed with couples in mind.

She couldn't believe how good the heat felt, or how amazing it was to have Alex join her. Especially when he pressed flush against her once more. She heard him doing something behind her, but she wasn't sure what until she heard a bottle squirt. He'd gotten the sponge and soaked it with coconut-scented wonderfulness. Not moving an inch, with his entire front plastered to her front, he washed her back. Slow circles, first the sponge, then his hand. It was the most sensual thing she'd ever felt. Almost as if they were part of each other.

The realization that she was here, with Alex, and this was actually happening, hit her again. Most of her days were spent focused on problems. Diagnosing illnesses, fixing broken bones, healing and teaching and finding ways to ease the pain of creatures who could not speak to her. She wasn't by any means a horse whisperer or pet psychic, yet she knew how to comfort, how to see what wasn't immediately apparent in a hurt creature. It wasn't magic, it was being open. Using her senses as best she knew how. It was science and it was concern, and to a large extent it was compassion that made her a good veterinarian. Yet she'd never been able to use any of these traits when it came to human males.

Until Alex.

It hadn't been immediate. Layer after layer had been

slowly peeled away as he became more forthcoming, as she became more willing.

The only thing that had made it possible at all was that they hadn't met. Hadn't even talked on the phone.

It was the computer that had given her the safety net of letting her guard down. And being with him in person threatened all they'd built.

She'd thought about canceling from the moment she'd logged off the night of her birthday.

Alex moved the sponge lower. Her eyes closed as he gently washed the curve of her bottom. But it was when his hand followed that she put her arms around his neck, her cheek on his chest, and let her body have its way.

His fingers were slippery with soap, the scent of coconut infused the moist air, and she parted her legs. She felt his cock twitch against her stomach as he touched her.

"Oh, my God," she whispered.

"You feel incredible," he said. "Everything about you makes me crazy."

"So my plan is working?"

His chest rose and fell with his chuckle. "You like making me insane, do you?"

"I do."

"Naughty, naughty."

She wiggled against him, knowing she was asking for trouble. But trouble sounded too good to pass up.

He slapped her ass, making her jump. Not hard. Just right. A little bit of ouch that morphed into tingles that spread like honey. He did it again, the other cheek. It was loud in the shower, with them both being so wet.

"You going to behave?"

She shook her head, then turned so her lips were against his chest, right next to his right nipple, but not touching it. "Did you see, Alex? Did you see the panties I had on?"

"I did."

"Do you know why I wore them?" she whispered.

"To please me?" he asked.

She nodded, then stuck out her tongue, licking up droplets.

He shifted and she knew he wanted her to lick his nipple. She didn't.

Both of his hands grabbed hold of her ass. He squeezed, lifting her, moving her to the right.

She laughed. Then she bit him. Yeah, right there. She tugged his hard little nub, loving that his groan made him vibrate.

"Either we get out of this shower and go to bed, or I'm gonna have to take care of some things right here."

"Some things?"

His hands moved from the back to the front. One finger slipped over her clit, then deep inside her. "Yeah. Things."

"Bed," she said, looking up.

He smiled. "Bed." He released her, reaching back to turn off the shower. Then he leaned out, grabbed a big bath sheet and draped it over her shoulders.

She dried herself as Alex got his own towel. She briefly considered fooling around with the towels and difficult-to-reach places, then had an inspired idea that would make him even crazier.

Dashing out of the bathroom, she said, "Give me a minute," before she closed the door. She went to the dresser, got another pair of white panties and slipped them on. She dropped the towel where she stood, then went to the end of the bed to wait.

The moment she heard the door open, she climbed onto the great big white comforter. On all fours, knowing he was watching every move she made, she crawled slowly up the mattress, amazed at her own boldness and the sensations coursing through her.

She'd never felt this powerfully sexual. Never known how much she could feel desired. She was someone else here, some other Meg.

The bed dipped behind her but she didn't turn. She just kept inching forward, moving her shoulders and her legs as if she were a cat, as if she were the most exotic creature in the world. Her hair dripped, some water inched down her sides and her shoulders, and that felt intoxicating, too. Everything was hypercharged, as if lightning were about to strike.

When his hands came down on her waist, she gasped. Gripping her tightly, he lifted her clear off the bed, then flipped her over onto her back. He straddled her, his eyes dark with lust.

Her gaze moved down his bare chest, which was heaving with his breaths, but didn't linger there. His cock, thick and weeping, caught and held her attention. She reached out with curious fingers, brushing the length of him.

He hissed as if she'd burned him. A flush of power made her grip him firmly and stroke down.

"You want this to be over now," he said, his voice practically a growl, "keep it up."

"I think it's staying up quite nicely by itself."

His look told her that humor was not going to win her major points. On the other hand, as hard as he was, she could pretty much do a riff on state birds, and he'd think it was the hottest thing since the blow job was invented.

But she decided not to torture him. Besides, he wasn't the only one who needed more. Now.

She let him go only to wiggle between his thighs.

He leaned down, bracing himself on corded arms, and kissed her again, hot and deep. Even as she moved to hold him, he pulled away, lying beside her.

"You're still wearing too many clothes," he said.

"What are you gonna do about it?"

He smiled, nipped her shoulder, then inched down, pausing at her chest. He leaned over her body, flicking her nipple. She arched into the sensation, but he teased her, moving back so that just the tip of his tongue touched her, pointed, snakelike, making her moan.

Too soon, he was on the move again, kissing her waist, then her hip, licking his way to the edge of her panties.

He grasped the material in his teeth and edged it downward. His sigh carried to her just before his fingers reached across her body to help.

Tugging, he whispered, "Up."

She lifted her hips, and the last of her clothes slid down her legs. Since she didn't want anything to stop the breathtaking stuff he was doing with his tongue, she used her toes to toss the panties away.

Naked now, suddenly aware that the bedside lamp was on and that she was on top of the covers, not hiding in any way, she boldly spread her legs in invitation.

His hand ran up the length of her inner thigh. "You're so beautiful."

"More," she said, meaning his touch, although if he wanted to call her wonderful things, she wasn't about to stop him.

"Don't worry. We'll get to everything."

"Promise?"

"You have my word."

He moved his hand up to the crease above her thigh, then he licked her, a long sweep of his tongue just above his thumb. "You taste like honey."

In fact, she did. She had this marvelous hand-milled honey soap that she'd bought for this very reason. Although she had to wonder if he was just waxing poetic, given the shower and all. It didn't matter. She felt as if she tasted like honey.

Her thoughts of soap were swept away when Alex moved between her legs. Now both hands explored the sensitive flesh there, and his breath warmed her mound.

His fingers brushed her gently, somewhere between a tickle and a caress. Something else she'd bought for the trip was her spankin' new Brazilian wax. Given the sensations ripping through her, it had been worth the price, and yeah, the pain.

"You okay?"

"Uh-huh. Why?"

"Well, maybe if you relaxed just a bit…"

She realized she had his head in a death grip between her thighs. "Sorry," she said, as she dropped her legs back to the mattress.

"Points for enthusiasm," he said, his voice filled with humor.

"Do you deduct for bodily injury?"

"Depends on what parts."

She laughed, but it turned into a gasp as he parted her lips and flicked her with his pointed tongue.

A low chuckle was quickly followed by an assault of the most amazing kind... He knew just where, how hard, and oh God.

Her hands fisted in the soft comforter and her muscles tensed. It had been so long. She closed her eyes and let the feelings take over. No thoughts except one—it was *Alex*.

Her breathing quickened as she felt the spark that was the beginning. Alone, she'd have stretched out, focused the vibrator in the perfect spot. A sound came out of her that was mostly a scream, but higher. When Alex stopped, stopped completely, it sure as hell became a scream.

He looked at her from between her thighs, his grin as wicked as his tongue. "Not yet," he said.

"Are you kidding me?"

Shaking his head slowly, he crawled up the length of her until he looked straight down. "I have other plans for you."

"What, you want to go square dancing?" she said.

"Not quite," he murmured.

"It'd better be good."

"Good isn't even close."

His hand went to her hair, where he gripped her, holding her steady. Then he leaned down and kissed her again.

She tasted herself, and it was raw and a little wicked, and her hips lifted in a thrust beyond her control.

His knee slipped between her legs, right up against her crotch. With every stab of his tongue, he pressed into her, reawakening the nerve endings he'd abandoned so callously.

She whimpered, because it felt so good and because it wasn't enough. His chuckle told her he understood, but that he wasn't going to rush things, not even if she begged.

God help her, it made her insane with wanting him. This game, this torture, it was all in his hands. He was playing her. What she didn't understand was how he knew what it would take to get her to this fever pitch. If she'd been asked exactly what she wanted, it wouldn't have been this. She wanted to come. Wasn't that the point? And yet…

He tugged at her hair, bringing her back from her thoughts. Forcing her to be *right there* as he took her mouth, as his knee pressed only so hard.

She bit him. Not badly, not so it would break the skin on his lower lip, just to remind him who he was dealing with here. He winced, dabbed the aching spot with a flick of his tongue. Then he smiled at her, as if she'd just done the most delightful trick.

"I knew it," he said.

"Knew what?" God, her voice was so breathless.

"That you, my dear Meg, are still undomesticated."

"Is that so?"

He sat back, moved his legs so he was next to her, not touching. "I pictured this moment a hundred times. Only my imagination fell incredibly short." He ran his hand down her arm, then to the shallow of her stomach. It rested there and his gaze didn't waver. "I wanted this. I prayed you wanted this, too, although if you hadn't…"

"You'd have wanted your money back?"

"Hell no. Don't you get it?" He looked at her again. "This is the icing. Magnificent icing, I'll admit, but no. The prize here is you. That I can make you shiver…"

She sat up, even though she didn't want his hand to go away. But she needed him to know this, and it didn't feel right lying down. "It's going to make things difficult, you know."

He nodded. "The only drawback."

"Worth it, though," she said.

"You think?"

She scooted closer to him. He was still erect, although not as fiercely as before. Which was only fair, because she was still thrumming with what he'd done to her. "Just know this," she said, touching his shoulder. "When we finish chatting, and it's very late, I'll crawl into bed with the memory of this. And when I close my eyes it won't be the vibrator I'm thinking about. Not some movie star, not an ex. It's going to be you. I want to remember everything we do here. The swimming and the eating and the volleyball. I sound like a Hallmark card, but it's true."

"Oh, yeah, the Masturbatory Memories line?"

She gave him the look. "Pinching will hurt much worse without your pants on."

He moved as if he was getting up. "I'd better go get them—"

She tackled him before he rose another inch. They fell back onto the pillows, his laughter as erotic as any touch.

"Too much, huh?" she said.

"What?"

She frowned. "I didn't mean to get all serious on you."

"You can be anything you want with me," he said.

"That's just because your dick is hard," she retorted.

"Hey, not true."

"Right. And the check is in the mail."

He turned so their faces were mere inches apart. "I think you're confusing me with someone else."

"You're a guy," she said.

He sighed. "Meg, remember the first time we talked, I mean that whole thing about the big bands?"

She nodded.

"Since that moment I haven't thought of you as anyone but Meg Becker. Not for a second."

Her face got warm and she lowered her eyes. "Sorry."

"It's okay. Just don't forget. I may do guy things, but I've never disappointed you. And I won't now."

"Okay, fair enough."

He lifted her chin with his fingers. "Five days, four nights. Nothing but fun and food and sex. Got it?"

"Got it."

"Now, where was I?"

"You said something about plans?" she said.

"Ah, that's right." His hands slipped between her legs, where his finger did evil things in the very best way.

She shifted until her head rested against his chest, near the crook in the arm he wasn't using.

He moved so gently it was like being slowly lowered into a warm bath. Her shoulders relaxed, her breathing calmed and she wanted this, only this, to go on forever.

He kissed her temple, and for some weird reason, tears came to her eyes. Maybe because it was so sweet, or maybe because that tender act was the thing she'd wanted most.

She couldn't remember the last tender moment she'd shared with a man. Hank hadn't been anything but fast and hard. He was the least sentimental man she'd ever known, which had worked well for her back then.

She was older now, and kindness had gone to the top of her wish list.

"What are you thinking?" Alex whispered, so close to her ear she felt the warmth of his breath.

"That you're nice."

"Ouch."

She turned a little to look at his face. He seemed pained. "What?"

"Nice? Is that any way to talk to the man who's got you in such a vulnerable position?"

"It was a compliment."

"Not from this side of the genetic pool."

She could tell it hadn't been too horrible a comment; his finger hadn't stopped. In fact, the pace was exactly the same. Mesmerizing. "I think I got past my bad boy phase during college," she told him. "The last thing I'm looking for in a friend or a lover is bad."

"Nope, too late. The die has been cast. I'm nice. Nice Alex. I'm sweet, too. Dammit."

"Okay, okay, you're a card-carrying asshole. I was so, so wrong. Don't hurt me," she teased.

He laughed. "Damn straight."

She snuggled closer, focusing more on her lower

parts. He just kept circling in that same way, with that one finger. Only the more she thought about it, the less she cared about relaxation.

As if he'd read her mind, the circles grew smaller, quicker. When she grasped his arm, he moved, but only so he could be more precise.

Meg's mouth opened but no sound came out. Nothing was happening now but tension. Her muscles, her pulse.

His other hand moved to hers and guided her down. She caught on quickly and slid over his flank until she found what she was looking for.

She circled him with her fingers, and while she meant to tease him, she couldn't. Instead, she matched his pace, running the length of him, which wasn't minor, from the base to the crown. Swiping her thumb across the head earned her a very succinct curse, but in a good way. She slicked him down again, knowing if he stopped this time she'd kill him.

Of course, he did, but before she could search for a weapon, he did that flipping thing again, which was something of a miracle, as she was no delicate flower. But there she was on her back, gasping as her whole body went straight to the brink of orgasm.

In another display of he-man strength, he lifted her thighs and butt and shoved one of the nice firm pillows underneath.

"Condoms," he said, and she completely understood the desperation in his voice.

"Drawer."

He leaned over, ripped the box apart, tore the package open with his teeth and hissed until it was on. Then he was ready, and lordy, she was more than ready, so thank God he didn't ease into her or any crap like that.

He took her. Hard.

She cried out with the sheer intensity, the rightness of having him inside her. Her legs wrapped high around his waist, and she arched to meet his next thrust.

Above her, he had that look, that man thing she loved watching, as if nothing existed on the planet but her. The world could have ended, and he wouldn't have missed a beat.

For that, she was incredibly grateful.

It was her last cogent thought. The animal took over and it was grunting, and pushing and aching and almost, almost...

She pulled the comforter up when it hit, and she was so loud the whole island could hear. But then, a few seconds later, he grimaced, braced, and when he came, he came loud, too.

Panting, still shuddering with pleasure, she watched him as he pulsed a few more times, as his facial muscles relaxed and he was able to focus.

"Wow," he said.

"I'll say," she muttered.

"I have to move," he told her.

"It's okay. Just don't go far."

"Not a problem." He eased out of her, then took care of a little business after he rolled to his side. A moment later he got rid of the pillow under her butt and lay down beside her. His arm went around her shoulder and she curled so close she could hear his heart beat.

"Holy crap," he said, a little hoarsely.

"Uh-huh." She smiled and just enjoyed the after-glow. He was better than the Alex she'd built in her head. In so many ways. Four more days weren't going to be enough. Not even close.

12

"ARE YOU SLEEPY?" ALEX ASKED.

Meg shifted in his arms. "Not really. Drained, yes, sleepy, no."

"Me neither."

"So," she murmured, looking up at him. "What do you want to do?"

He shrugged. "Staying in bed is good. Or we could go dancing. Or check out the cove."

"Or we could go back to the Trade Winds and have some of that key lime pie."

He nodded. "Mmm, pie."

"It means getting up," she said.

"Showering," he added.

"Putting on clothes."

"I was with you right up to that putting on clothes thing," he said.

She sat up, flipped her wild hair behind her shoulders. "I must have pie."

"And so you shall." He got up and held his hand out for hers. She stood, kissed him and led him to the bathroom.

She got the towels, he turned on the water. He wished

he was seventeen again so that he could take advantage of all that warm water and slippery soap, but instead, he just washed her beautiful back and admired the scenery.

When it was her turn with the sponge, she took her time, rubbing his shoulders with care. His eyes closed and he hummed in satisfaction.

"Alex?"

"Hmm?"

"I'm sorry about inviting Tina and Walter to dinner."

"You didn't. They invited themselves," he stated.

"But I didn't even try to get us out of it."

The sponge moved to the middle of his back, and he realized that while the professional masseuse had been skilled, adept and very good at her job, being washed by Meg was in a class by itself.

"I felt sorry for her," she said.

"Why sorry? Because her husband is so consumed with his work that he can't see her?"

Her hand stilled. "Well, yeah."

Alex turned to face her, even though it meant she wouldn't be washing his lower back. "You only felt sorry for her?"

"You said it yourself. He can't see her," she said.

"He can't see anything but his job. Sound familiar?"

"This is not about me," she said defensively.

"If you say so," he replied.

Her face scrunched up. "Stop that. You don't get it about the mountain. It's not like a regular job."

"I know. A regular job would let you breathe a little. You might actually find yourself a life," he said.

"Don't be blithe about this, Alex. It's not fair."

He heard the hurt in her voice. "I'm sorry. I'm being a jerk. Not that I didn't warn you, but still. I'm sorry."

She hit him weakly with her balled fist, and then she stepped out of the shower, grabbing one of the white fluffy towels.

He felt like shit. Couldn't he just keep his self-righteous mouth shut? Meg was strong and smart and she knew her own life. Just because he'd decided to change his path didn't mean she had to. Although, if she couldn't...

He rinsed off and followed her into the other room, wrapping his towel around his waist.

She was standing by the closet, holding a red dress still on the hanger.

He padded across the wood floor until he was just behind her. With both hands on her slender shoulders, he leaned down. "We okay?"

She turned. "I know you're concerned, but honestly, I'm all right. When we get online, I'm exhausted and frustrated, and I bitch to you. I don't talk about the good parts. The people I care about. The animals I've helped."

"It must be great."

She smiled. "Pie now?"

"I'll be right down. And I think you'll look gorgeous in that dress."

CHARLIE HANOVER WALKED OUT OF the hotel lobby, trying to get his anger under control. It didn't help that his flight had been a nightmare, but now that he was here, no one would give him Alex's room number, and he couldn't find Butch Castellano, the owner of Escapades, who would. His buddy in Washington had convinced Castellano to find a room for Charlie, which was great, but if he couldn't locate Alex, the favor was useless.

The damn place was huge and he didn't have a clue where to start. He'd gotten Alex's cell number, but it went right to voice mail every time he called.

He'd already checked out the pools, the disco, a couple of restaurants and the spa. The problem was, Rosten could be in his room, he could be on a boat or at the beach. There was simply too much territory to cover, and it was already eleven.

Charlie walked past the fountain at the top of the steps, then down to the wide path where his cart waited. It felt absurd to set off at random, so when he had started the cart he headed for the north side of the hotel, toward his room. He had to strategize. Tomorrow, he'd go to room service. Surely Rosten had ordered something, and Charlie felt certain he could bribe some of the wait staff to send him in the right direction.

He would also spread some dough to housekeeping, maybe the spa. No way in hell was he leaving this island without an exclusive.

From his latest phone calls, he'd learned the shit was definitely hitting the fan in D.C. He knew it was going to be a big story when he got word that the *Daily Show* had put out an APB to get Alex on the air. Competing, of course, with CNN, Fox News and PBS *NewsHour,* not to mention the news royalty—the nightly news shows.

Charlie still couldn't believe what he'd read in the columns, but he wondered if those outside the circle would get the significance of the act. It was as if the head of the Freemasons had given out the secret handshake to all and sundry. It simply wasn't done.

The big question was why? Why talk about that most sacrosanct of procedures, the very underpinning of how Washington worked, in such a public forum? Alex must have realized he'd never write in the town again. Who would trust him?

True, the man hadn't quite crossed the line. None of his sources had been officially off the record. The only trouble anyone would get into from the revelations were those who'd been less than forthright in their dealings with the American people, like Senator Allen. Which, Charlie figured, was the point. And Alex hadn't spared himself. His sins were now part of the public record.

An interesting, if foolhardy, move. One usually reserved for those who had nothing left to lose. And that's what Charlie wanted to find out. Why would a man as young and successful as Alex Rosten throw his career away? What did he hope to accomplish?

As Charlie neared the north hotel entrance, he found his musings had gotten him too wired to sleep. He turned the electric cart around and headed back to the crowds. Who knows, maybe he'd get lucky.

THIS TIME, Meg made sure they got a table for two. It was after eleven, but there were still a lot of people eating dinner. She loved that there were folks in bathing suits eating lobster sitting next to a couple in formal wear eating a large platter of French fries. Vacations were good things.

She smiled at Alex, who was looking quite yummy

in a pale gray silk shirt and jeans. She tried to picture him in his suit and tie, all Washington proper. He'd look great, but there was something so incredibly sexy about his casual clothes that made her want to rub against his body like a cat.

"Key lime pie, huh? You don't want to look at the rest of the desserts?"

She shook her head. "When I find something I like, I stick with it."

Alex quirked his head. "Are we talking about sweets here?"

"We most definitely are," she said, as she slipped her foot out of her sandal and ran her toe under the hem of his jeans.

His smile came slowly as his eyes narrowed wickedly.

"I meant to tell you when we were in the bungalow," she said, leaning forward, her finger skimming the rim of her water glass.

"Tell me what?" Alex asked.

"You know that loft upstairs?"

He nodded.

"You won't be using that," she said.

"I see."

"If that's okay with you," she added.

"I think we can come to some sort of agreement."

"You do, huh?" she teased.

"You don't snore, do you?" he teased back.

"What if I did?"

He grinned. "Wouldn't make a damn bit of difference." He leaned closer. "I was just trying to be all dark and mysterious. Inside I was wagging my tail like a puppy."

She laughed as the waitress came to their table.

"The lady wishes to have key lime pie," Alex said.

"And for you?" the waitress asked.

"Oh, I want that, too."

"And to drink?" the waitress added.

Meg put her hand on Alex's, just because. "I'll have iced tea, please."

The waitress turned to Alex.

"You have whole milk?" he asked.

She nodded.

"That's great."

With a smile, the waitress left to fill their order, while Meg stared at Alex. "Milk?"

"What's the matter with milk?" he said.

"Nothing. It does a body good."

"Hey, I'll need all my strength if I'm not sleeping upstairs," he stated.

"I'm not even sure you're going to be sleeping downstairs," she quipped.

"Maybe I'll have two glasses of milk."

Meg squeezed his hand. "I love innuendos. And double entendres."

"I'll do my best to keep up the pace," he said.

"You're doing fine," she told him.

"You know what you can do for me?" he said, smiling.

"What?"

"Tell me about the good parts."

"Of sex?" she asked, although she knew what he meant the minute the words were out of her mouth. "Oh, you mean work."

He nodded. "I'd like to know."

"The critters," she said. "Above everything, I love the animals more than I can say. And being on the mountain lets me grow up with them, not just see them once and off they go. I deliver the babies. I fix them when they get sick. I bury them, too, but that's not as bad as you'd think. They're all mine on some level, and that's an amazing thing. I can't think of another vet that has what I do."

"Wow," Alex said, leaning back in his chair. "I never thought about it that way. I can see where it would be fulfilling."

She nodded. "The llamas at O'Reilly's place can be major pains in the ass. But there are these twins that I've known since day one, and every time I come by, they can't get enough of me. They're like puppies the way they follow me around. And when I leave, they watch until my truck is out of sight. It's pretty cool."

"I'm envious. We never had pets growing up. Allergies. And then I was in college, and life got crazy. I've always wanted a dog," he said.

"You're allergic?" she asked.

"No. Most of the rest of my family is. So pets weren't allowed. Although I did have a pet frog for a few weeks. He couldn't fetch worth a damn," Alex joked.

She chuckled and brightened as she caught sight of their pie. She couldn't look away as the waitress walked across the room, but Meg heard a couple of "oohs" in her wake.

Each slice was huge. Enough for two, easily. Not that Meg was willing to share. And she could see that the whipped cream was the real thing, made fresh moments ago.

It looked so good, she didn't even wait for her iced tea to hit the table. She tasted the first bite and swooned. The bright lime flavor burst across her tongue, and her eyes closed out of sheer bliss.

"Oh, my God," Alex said, his words muffled because his mouth was full.

She nodded. If anyone tried to take one crumb from her plate, she'd stab him to death with her fork. Luckily, no evil threatened, and she slowly, bite by exquisite bite, made her way through the pie. As she neared the end, her bites got smaller and smaller because she didn't want it to end.

She had four more days to enjoy Escapades. Which meant four more pieces of this amazing treat.

"Oh, shit."

She looked up, surprised at Alex's vehemence, although she understood. But he wasn't talking about the fact that he'd already finished his pie. He was staring over the edge of the deck, watching a golf cart drive slowly by.

"What?" she asked, looking at the driver. He was an average-looking man, a little chunky and balding, but about the same age as Alex.

"I have to get out of here."

"Why? What's wrong?" she demanded.

"Charlie Hanover, that's what's wrong," he said tersely.

"Who?"

"He writes for the *New York Times*, and I know he's not here on vacation."

"How can you possibly know that?" she asked.

"Because I know him, and I have no doubt whatsoever that he's looking for me. We've known each other since college, and there's no love lost between us. I caught him in some nasty dealings back in the day, and he's never forgiven me."

"What does he want?"

"To make sure I never write another column. That I'm disgraced. The man is nothing if not vindictive."

"You don't want to confront him?"

"Not here. I know I'm going to have to run the gauntlet when I get back, but I'm on vacation. Charlie can wait, just like all the others," Alex stated. "Ah, you've finished your dessert. Perhaps it wouldn't be so bad if we moved this to, say, the beach?"

"Or, say, the disco?"

"Seriously?" he asked.

"I just ate a billion calories. I need to move," she said, patting her stomach.

"We could go back to the bungalow."

"We will. But later. Let's at least check it out, okay?"

"Whatever you want." He held her chair for her as she struggled not to eat the last crumb on her plate.

The elevator for the disco was right outside the restaurant entrance. Alex got very James Bond looking for the reporter guy as they walked the short distance.

It was so curious to her. He talked about these columns so casually, as if they were nothing, and yet, from his brief description earlier today, she knew they were anything but. Especially since a reporter from the *New York Times* had flown here just to track down Alex.

"Alex?" she murmured as she hit the up button on the elevator.

"Yes?"

"When do I get to read these columns?"

"Figured you'd ask. And I want you to read them. Only, not yet, okay?"

"Before we leave?"

"Yeah. I promise."

"Great, thanks." She wouldn't push it, but she'd make sure he kept his word.

The ride was short, just long enough for a kiss that made her toes curl. Then the doors opened right onto the disco.

The joint was hopping. The band, which was really large and included horns along with guitars, keyboard and drums, was on a stage at the back. There were tables on two levels, and a big dance floor flooded with colored lights and happy people.

Alex led her to a table near the bar, which was a total score, and a moment later a waitress in a very skimpy skirt and bikini top came by. Meg ordered a Sex on the Beach. Alex, on the other hand, went with a Coke. Huh.

He leaned over, resting his hand on her shoulder. "Do you want to dance?"

She leaned his way. "What?"

He got closer. "Want to dance?"

"What?"

He moved his mouth right up to her ear, so close his breath made her quiver. "Dance?"

She nodded.

Alex stood, but when she joined him, she leaned over to his ear. Just as close. "I heard you the first time."

His brows furrowed. "What?"

This time, she licked the shell of his ear with the tip of her tongue. "I heard you the first time."

His head turned, fast, and his hand darted up to hold her by the back of the neck. He kissed her. Hard.

It was a good thing he was holding her, too, because, damn. When he finally pulled back, he smiled. "I know."

She pinched him.

"Ow."

With a wicked grin, she headed for the dance floor. Alex followed closely. They found a spot to call their own and she began to move. It had been forever since she'd danced. Her most frequent partner was Ellen DeGeneres, but that didn't happen often, because Meg wasn't home when the show came on. As for partners that weren't talk show hosts, there'd been...

She couldn't even remember.

Alex moved, too. He didn't go crazy, but he knew what a beat was and knew how to feel it. It shouldn't have surprised her. She knew what he listened to, and if that didn't mean he had soul, nothing would.

He'd told her he liked to sing along with Ella Fitzgerald, but that he never sang in public because while he had the passion, he didn't have the chops.

It wasn't the naughtiest of his revelations, but it was one that had given Meg a good clue as to who he was. Although she had to wonder what she truly did know about him, after today's revelations. She could still hardly believe that he'd told her so little about his work life. Perhaps it had something to do with the amount of time she'd spent bitching about hers. That was something she'd think about later, when she wasn't on a dance floor.

The song was something she didn't recognize, although she'd wager it was originally done by Earth, Wind and Fire. The horn section rocked, the whole band was fabulous and her body felt deliciously loose after the massage. But it ended too soon. She was just getting started.

"I'll be right back," Alex said.

She nodded and watched him head for the restrooms. She waited for the music to start again. When it did, she grinned. "Get the Party Started." That one, she knew.

Even though Alex was still away, she danced. Danced her ass off. Just closed her eyes and let it go, because this wasn't the real world and she couldn't have cared less what anyone thought. Despite her determination to think of nothing but the here and now, thoughts about their earlier conversations refused to leave her be.

He talked to her all the time, even when she wasn't there. That had been a shocker. Not just because he'd confessed to the somewhat odd behavior, but because she talked to him, too. Talked. Cried on his shoulder. Made love to him. All in her head. Only tonight it had become real, and she didn't have to pretend at all. The reality surpassed the fantasy beyond any expectation or hope.

She laughed as the music filled her senses and then oh, God, Alex's hand was on hers, pulling her close.

They moved together as if they'd done it forever. They touched, hand to hand, hip to hip, and, by the end, groin to groin.

She felt that thing again, like when they'd had that moment in the bar. She wished they could go on like this forever, but this song ended, too.

They stumbled back to their table to find the drinks already there. After a few breathless minutes, Alex scooted close, put his hand on her thigh. "This is good."

"Very good."

"I mean us. In person. Live and in color."

"Yeah, I heard you the first time."

His grin was crooked, and very sweet. She leaned forward and kissed him gently on the lips.

He didn't keep it gentle. His mouth opened wider and his tongue dipped inside, tasting, teasing. For long moments, with the sound of the music and chatter all around, she just melted into him. Making out like they were in the backseat of an old Chevy. He moaned as his hand slipped under the hem of her dress, and she thought about how it had been have him inside her. Incredible.

She wanted Alex. All of him. Naked and on the soft bed, with nothing to stop them from exploring every fantasy they'd ever talked about.

She squeezed her legs together as she remembered one particularly intense late-night conversation. He'd asked her if she ever wanted to explore her darker side. She'd never told another living soul that she even had one, but he'd confessed some pretty dark stuff himself, and, well, she did wonder about things.

Not that she necessarily wanted to try them for real. But maybe, with someone like Alex, she could dip her toe into the water.

That whole spanking thing. It wasn't something

she thought a lot about. When she did, though, she imagined herself tied and helpless. Very exposed. Very aroused.

She moaned, her legs parting for his fingers. But when he touched her inner thigh, she came back to herself. To where they were. She pulled away.

He stilled. "You okay?"

She nodded.

"Sorry." He brushed her hair over her shoulder. "Truth is, you make me forget myself."

"I know what you mean. But I think I've gotten that exhibitionist streak out of my system. In fact, I'm thinking it might be nice to do some private things."

"Dammit." He looked away, his jaw set and his mouth tight.

"You have an objection?"

He looked back at her. "Are you kidding? I'm dying to do all kinds of private things, but I did something."

"Now you're starting to scare me."

"Not a bad thing. Just one that's going to keep us here for a little while."

She couldn't imagine what he was talking about.

"I'll see if I can cancel—"

The band was back and the singer was at the mike. "This one's for Meg," he said.

Her eyes widened. "Me, Meg?"

Alex got that crooked smile again. "You, Meg."

"Cool."

The music started, and then she really got it. The tune was "In the Mood," the Glen Miller standard, which they both loved to pieces.

"Can you do it?" Alex asked.

"Oh, yeah."

He stood, held out his hand, and they went to the middle of the dance floor. The problem was her dress. It was too tight to do this properly. But the hell with it. After all, she'd been dancing to this music since she was a little kid.

He pulled her onto the floor and immediately into a spin. It was just like dancing with her father, only a million times better because Alex moved like a born hepcat. And it was Alex.

Despite the tightness of her dress, she didn't do too badly. In fact, the other folks made room for them, and some even stopped dancing just to watch.

Meg felt as if she were in a movie, and that Alex was the sexiest, most wonderful leading man ever. When the song finally ended, they were both panting and laughing from the pure exhilaration of it all.

He looked into her eyes. "Happy?"

"More than I could have ever guessed."

His gaze darted across her face as he brushed her cheek with the back of his hand. "I know." He kissed her gently, then smiled. "Let's go home."

13

THEY'D TAKEN the golf cart to the restaurant instead of walking, and after dancing, Alex was grateful. He wanted to get back to the bungalow, back to bed.

For the lateness of hour, the traffic was crazy. Nothing, it seemed, closed at the hotel, or even the spa, if the lights were any indication. He wondered how many people it took to run a place like this. And where the locals lived.

"That was a wonderful treat," Meg said. "I'm surprised they knew the song."

He touched her hand as he maneuvered past couples on the path. "I was, too, but they did a great job. You sure can cut a rug."

"I loved it. Did I tell you my parents won a dancing contest when they were dating? They got a trophy and everything."

"Oh, shit. Hang on." Alex jerked the cart into a hard right, then another, narrowly avoiding a palm tree, steering them back toward the hotel.

Meg squealed as she grabbed on for dear life, but Alex could only spare her a glance as he weaved his way among the bicycles and pedestrians.

He felt sure Charlie had spotted him, and he wished there was a rearview mirror on this thing so he could see if Hanover had turned to make chase.

Making sure there was no one immediately in front of him, Alex kept his foot on the pedal as he looked behind him. Although his quick glance didn't let him see the man's face, he did see a cart speeding after them.

"Is it him?"

Alex nodded. "Dammit, I don't want to do this. I'm going to try and lose him."

Meg held on to the side panels of the door with both hands. "Maybe I could talk to him. Let him know that I'm pretty damn good at the whole gelding thing."

"That sounds like fun, but no," he replied. "I don't want you to talk to him. He'd hammer you until you told him something you didn't want him to know."

"That's ridiculous, Alex. I can turn around and walk away."

"You're brilliant, Meg, but you've never been subjected to anything like Charlie Hanover. He's brought heads of state to tears. Seriously, it's not worth it."

"It's an island, Alex. Where is there to go?"

"We'll find out."

"You're enjoying this, aren't you?"

He deftly passed a slow-moving cart, making sure no one had to step on the brakes. "Enjoying being chased all over an island in an electric cart with a gorgeous woman at my side? Naw."

Meg laughed, and for that he was grateful. If she'd been pissed, he'd have ended the game, told Charlie to go to hell, and, if he had to, gotten security to ensure their privacy. But, as Meg had so astutely noticed, this was much more fun.

He drove as if he were at the Grand Prix, only at about fifteen miles per hour. Meg got into the swing of things by shouting warnings at those up ahead. She even took point, looking back to mark Charlie's progress in the chase.

Finally, way past the brightest lights of the hotel, they came to a crossroads. Alex turned off the lights and veered left, toward the sea. He had to slow down, but there were fewer obstacles than they'd faced on the other end of the path.

If he remembered correctly, this would lead them to the cove. He had no idea whether Charlie was following and Meg couldn't tell. She'd shifted in the seat so she could look for him, but if he was on their tail, he'd doused his beams, too.

They drove on, getting yelled at a couple of times for driving without headlights. Alex didn't mind. He liked it even better when Meg scooted closer, abandoning her lookout, and took his hand in hers.

The full moon made it possible to keep going until they neared the cliffs. The path ended there, and Alex didn't want to do something bad to the electric cart, so he pulled off the road. When he cut the motor, they just sat for a few long minutes, waiting.

In the quiet, the sound of the waves washing against a hidden shoreline made him forget about Charlie, newspapers, the rest of the world. The only thing that mattered was the woman next to him, who'd slipped her hand from his grasp to his thigh.

He pulled her into a kiss, letting himself sink into the soft heat of her mouth. Time slowed as her tongue teased in the most leisurely fashion, even as his heart beat urgently.

She pulled back suddenly with a sound of distress.

"What's wrong?"

"This isn't the back seat of a stretch limo."

"I'm pretty sure we've lost him. Let's go back to the bungalow."

"He's probably waiting for us to do just that. We still have the towels in the back, don't we?"

He leaned to kiss her again. "Why, Ms. Becker, I do believe you're a genius."

"Not quite. We don't have other necessary accoutrements."

"Oh, right."

"But making out is fun."

"It is, indeed."

CHARLIE LOOKED AT his watch one more time. His eyes burned with fatigue, his butt hurt from sitting in the damn cart, and not one vehicle had come this way for at least a half hour. "Screw it."

He turned around and headed back to the hotel. He'd found Alex once, he'd do it again. In fact, he was sorry now he hadn't just gone with his original plan.

The one thing he knew now that he didn't before was that Alex hadn't come here alone. Was the woman behind his decision to spill the beans? Charlie would have to do some more digging. He hadn't recognized her, although admittedly he hadn't gotten a good look, but something told him she was involved. Which made his journalistic heart skip a beat.

Adding sex to the mix was a fantastic bonus.

MEG STEPPED OUT of the cart and up the stairs to the bungalow, not waiting for Alex. Talk about foreplay. For an hour, they'd spread out on the beach, comfortable on the two towels, and made out like teenagers. She hadn't done that since forever, and it had been heaven.

Just kissing him was something she could do for a living. She'd always loved to kiss, but she'd never met anyone who met her high standards as well as Alex did.

His hands and hers had wandered, but they'd never unzipped anything or snuck under anything, which somehow had made it all sexier.

Now, she dashed into the bathroom to get herself ready for phase two. It was late, but she didn't care. Every one of her erogenous zones screamed for immediate attention.

It took her only a few minutes to brush her teeth and her hair. She thought about undressing, but decided to see what Alex was up to.

She walked out to find him bent over the bed, wearing nothing but boxers, pulling down the comforter. Her eyes widened as she saw the lump under the covers that was her vibrator. He hadn't noticed it…yet. She cleared her throat and when he turned, she unzipped her dress and let it fall to the floor.

His moan made her whole body tremble.

HE WOKE, not remembering when he'd fallen asleep. Meg was still curled in the crook of his shoulder, her leg over his, her softness pressed against his thigh. He was grateful the light was still on so he could see her like this.

What he felt… Okay, so this was unexpected. Maybe not. He'd built up this meeting for a long time. It was natural that he'd brought a lot to the bedroom, a lot of fantasies.

The night breeze fluttered the gauzy white curtains, giving him glimpses of the darkness outside. He had no idea what time it was, which was somewhat disorienting.

In D.C., he always knew the time. His watch, the clock on his nightstand, the time stamp on his computer. Time ruled him in the real world. Time and deadlines. The weekly column that he'd wanted so badly he'd have killed for it had turned into something he'd never expected. He'd also had ideals back then, a naiveté that felt astonishing. Of course, there had been perks. Politicians curried his favor. He had access, he had power, he had privilege. All of which had hidden the poison apple he'd been only too happy to bite.

He tried to remember the last time he'd truly relaxed. Even when he was on vacation, work was always there. He never went anywhere without his cell phone, his computer, his contacts. He'd been consumed with his insular world, giving only half an eye to anything outside. It didn't matter if he was in Cannes or Sundance, the scenery mattered only in his search for a relay tower so he could get reception on his phone. Some life.

This week was all his. He'd left everything he'd been obsessed with behind, and it was only natural that he'd glommed on to Meg as the avatar of all that was free-dom and release.

On the other hand, holy shit.

He looked back down at the sleeping woman. Her hair was all over the place, and he pushed back a thick strand resting on her cheek, careful not to touch her, because if he did, he wasn't sure he could stop.

It had been a long time since he'd been with a woman who stirred him like Meg. As much as he'd cared for Ellen, they didn't exactly have fireworks in the bedroom. The other women he'd known had been good, fine. He'd had no complaints.

Meg was different. The only problem was, he wasn't sure if the difference was real.

Which was probably a good thing. His life was waiting for him, right where he'd left it. The good, the bad, the chaos. And whether he'd land on his feet or his ass was uncertain until he returned.

He reached for the lamp on the table, and just as he turned it off, Meg shifted. He froze, not wanting to wake her.

"Alex?" she said, her voice fuzzy from sleep.

"It's late. Go back to sleep."

"'Kay."

He tucked her closer, then reached across her body and grabbed the comforter. Now that the light was off, he didn't mind covering her up, especially since he could feel so much of her.

"Alex?"

He smiled. "Yes?"

"I was thinking," she murmured.

"About?"

"This is the best vacation ever."

"I'm glad."

She sniffled. Moved her leg higher up his thigh. And that was it. The end of the conversation. He could feel her slow, steady breaths brush his chest, and he realized that sleeping with Meg was better than anything he could think of. It was the best vacation ever. And way, way too short.

MEG WOKE BEFORE ALEX DID. She quickly reached under the covers and got her vibe, which lay exactly where she'd left it. It was going into her suitcase, not the drawer, because she really didn't need it now. After making sure Alex was still asleep, she snuck into the shower, hoping she wouldn't wake him. She wished she could have slept longer herself, but she was used to waking with the sun.

Her shower made her aware of some interesting aches, and also a couple of hickies on her neck. Hickies! She hadn't had one since seventh grade. Now all she needed was the prune skin to go with it. She'd never had so many showers in such a short period of time.

As she stepped out of the spray, Alex opened the door. "You done?"

"It's all yours."

"Good, because breakfast is going to be here in about ten minutes," he said.

"Here? Seriously?"

"They have golf carts that have small ovens in the back, so they can bring hot meals to the bungalows."

"That's good of them," Meg said, heading to the other room to get dressed. Her hair was still damp, after only a towel rub, but she didn't think she was going to take the time for a blow dry. The air would be enough, and after breakfast they were going to the cove, so she'd just get it wet again. What she did do was put on her bathing suit, slip her sundress on over that, then sneak back into the bathroom to grab her comb.

Alex was singing. "My Funny Valentine." It made her heart melt just a little bit more.

Stepping to the door, she checked herself in the full-length mirror. Not bad. Her bathing suit straps didn't even show. This cover-up had been an impulse buy, but now she was glad for it. Almost two hundred bucks for not a lot of material. It wrapped around her neck, then fell to just this side of midthigh. The pattern was bright—turquoise and tangerine flowers, with a hint of white. It made her feel sexy. Or was that Alex?

She went back into the main room and straightened the bed. Then she opened all the drapes. Just as Alex walked in wearing his trunks, she heard a cart drive up outside. They looked at each other—what if it was Charlie? Thankfully, it wasn't. It was two waiters, bearing food.

Alex let the waiters in. Two of them, both with the Escapades shirts, both with big smiles, as if serving them breakfast was the highlight of their day.

Whatever the management was doing here with the resort, they were doing it right. Every staff member she'd met had been cheerful, and not the kind of cheerful where you know they secretly would like to drown you in the pool, either.

She went over to investigate the treats that Alex had ordered, the polished wood cool and smooth under her bare feet. Champagne and orange juice caught her eye first. "Oh, mimosa cocktails. Very decadent."

Alex waggled his brows. "Wait."

The waiters had put all manner of dishes and glasses and silverware on the round table by the big window. With the drapes open, all she could see was blue ocean, blue sky. Dragging her eyes away from the spectacular view, she grinned at the tall vase filled with pink roses that had appeared in the center of the table. She looked at Alex.

"Hey," he said. "It's Valentine's Day."

"You sentimental sap," she said with delight.

"Wow, that's just what Dick Cheney called me last week. I guess I can't hide my softer side, huh?" he said, grinning at her.

She laughed, wanting very much to be alone with this man.

Her wish came true a few minutes later. Silver-domed plates, four of them, couldn't be left unexplored. The first one hid Belgian waffles, steaming hot. The second, eggs Benedict, which was her favorite thing, except for waffles. The third, cottage fries. When she reached for the fourth, Alex's hand stopped her.

"That's dessert."

She pulled back. He kissed her shoulder, then pulled out her chair. After she sat, he went to the champagne bucket.

"Cocktail, mademoiselle?"

"*Oui, merci,*" she said.

The champagne cork popped and the bubbly overflowed into the ice. Once it was under control, he poured two glasses, then added the OJ. He stirred with a long silver spoon.

He kissed her right before he handed her her drink.

Then he served her breakfast. The waffle got its own plate. The eggs and potatoes looked fabulous, and, rude as it was, she couldn't wait. Her hunger had reached critical levels, and she figured it was every man for himself.

Alex didn't seem to mind, although he prepared his waffle first.

"Got enough butter on that, Alex?"

"It's my vacation." He grinned, then poured an enormous amount of syrup over the waffle. "Vacations. Good."

By the time they were both stuffed, they'd also both had two mimosas. And yet he poured them each another glass, half-full, champagne only.

"Dessert," he said.

"Oh my God, I forgot. I ate too much."

"It's all right. Just see what it is."

She sighed, but she obeyed. She lifted the last of the domes. On the plate, on a brilliant blue napkin, was a silver charm. He'd bought her a charm. She'd had her bracelet for years. Her mother had given it to her on her sixteenth birthday, and she had mostly animal charms, but also one of a saxophone, and one of a little book, because of how she loved to read. She'd mentioned it to Alex aeons ago; she couldn't even remember the conversation or what had made her bring it up. His charm, her new favorite charm, was a tiny little record.

She picked it up and held it in the palm of her hand. "Oh, Alex."

"I know it's hard to see the label, but it's Tommy Dorsey. I promise."

She looked at him, then at the charm. It was stunning and it was the most thoughtful thing… "All I got you was white panties."

He burst out laughing. "Best present ever."

"I do my best."

"Perfect," he said, but it was a whisper, and she didn't think he was talking about underwear.

14

MEG THANKED THE NICE MAN behind the counter and turned to Alex. "All you have to do is breathe through the snorkel. And look at all the pretty fish."

Alex didn't seem convinced. He gazed at the yellow snorkel as if it would suddenly sprout teeth. "Fish, huh?"

"You know—fins, gills, bright colors."

He looked at her, then at the face mask in his other hand before he returned his gaze to the snorkel. "What's to prevent the water from entering the top, and coming into my mouth?"

Meg turned her face while she struggled not to laugh out loud. Thank God they hadn't gone scuba diving. The man was wonderful, but Jacques Cousteau he wasn't. Laughing at him, however, was not going to encourage him in the least, so she coughed quickly then turned back with a smile. "Well, see, you don't go very deep. You swim just under the surface, so you can watch through your mask, and the snorkel lets you keep on breathing. It's the best of both worlds."

He nodded, his expression still serious. "That makes sense. Where are the best fish to see?"

"It'd be difficult not to find great fish here, but the cove is supposed to be the prime spot."

"Let's hit it."

He sounded so determined that this time she did laugh. "Okay, Mr. *Sea Hunt*, let's do it."

They left the cabana where they'd gotten the equipment, only after standing in a considerable line, and returned to their golf cart. Meg felt as if she'd won the grand prize and the world was hers. Life would have been perfect if they hadn't had to look over their shoulders all the time.

Alex wore another pair of blue trunks today, different design, same blue. And this great striped shirt that hung loosely in just the right way. Even his feet looked sexy in his manly flip-flops. Altogether delicious.

They rounded the fountain on the steps and almost ran into a very tall, very bald man wearing long pants, no shirt and a large dragon tattooed on his arm. He bowed slightly and stepped out of their way. Just behind him was another man, many inches shorter, quite a few years older, and surprisingly elegant.

He smiled with even white teeth that matched his shirt as he held out his hand to Alex. "Butch Castellano," he said in a rough, New York baritone. "I hope you're having a good time."

"Excellent, thank you. I'm Alex Rosten, and this is Meg Becker."

The man turned to her. "Are they treating you well?"

"Like a queen."

"That's what I like to hear. You need anything, you

call me. Just ask for Mr. Castellano when you pick up the phone."

"There is one thing," Alex said.

Mr. Castellano's brows rose. "Yes?"

"There's a man here, a reporter. His name is Charlie Hanover and he works for the *New York Times*."

Castellano nodded.

"I'd appreciate it if no one at the hotel told him we're staying in the bungalows. This is our vacation, and he doesn't seem to understand the meaning of the word."

"I'll do what I can, Mr. Rosten. Everyone deserves a nice vacation."

Alex shook his hand once more. "Thank you."

As she led Alex to the steps, the big guy bowed again. Nothing extravagant, but a bow nonetheless.

"That was interesting," she said, as they got into their cart.

"That was Butch Castellano."

"So I gathered."

"He owns the place. And, of course, that explains the lobby."

"Huh?"

Alex started the cart and they went slowly down the path, heading toward the cove. It was a far piece from the hotel, and even farther from their bungalow, but that was okay. They passed couple after couple, and she stared like a tourist at each one. "He used to be in the mob."

"Really?"

"Yep. Spent a lot of years in jail for it. Some people said he took the fall for some big-time boss, but I never got any confirmation. After prison, he made some legit money on the ponies and parlayed that into real estate and good stock investments. Then he bought this island."

"And the lobby?"

"He collects art. French Impressionists are his field," Alex explained.

"So those paintings are real?" Meg squealed.

"I'm thinking yes," he said.

"Wow. No wonder he has his own personal Terminator."

"Oh, yeah. Never leaves home without one," he said.

"Must be tough."

Alex turned to her. "You must do okay financially. You're sure busy enough."

She smiled, although it was more ironic than joyful. "Ah, the wonderful folks on the mountain, while true blue to their myriad animals, are notoriously bad with their payments. I am the recipient, however, of a great number of cakes, cookies, pies and casseroles."

"So you work like a dog and get paid in biscuits?" he quipped.

She laughed. "That's one way of putting it."

"How would you?"

She looked past the beautiful people to the ocean beyond. There were white, wispy clouds in a perfect sky, and she didn't want to think about home. "It's my job. They count on me."

"Who do you count on?"

IN THE DAYLIGHT, the cove was one of the most beautiful places Alex had ever seen. Gorgeous cliffs were covered in brilliant green bushes and tropical plants, the water was so blue it seemed almost fake, and the white tips of the ocean rolled onto perfect sand in gentle waves.

Unfortunately, a whole lot of other guests had gotten the memo, because he and Meg were most definitely not alone. Although, luckily, there was still no sign of Hanover. Alex leaned over after she'd put her slinky dress on her towel. After a moment's silent thanks for whoever had invented the bikini, he asked, "Aren't there good fish by our bungalow?"

"Yes," she whispered back, "but not the *best* fish."

He grinned, then put his face mask on. Wrong.

"Uh, let me just…" She straightened it out. And then, even though he looked quite goofy, she kissed him. Maybe because he looked goofy.

She put on her mask, kicked off her sandals and grabbed his hand. It wasn't wall-to-wall tourists, but they had to walk a little to find a good open space to be alone. She sat down to put her fins on, but he tried it standing. Eventually, he sat, too, although not very delicately.

It wasn't easy putting the snorkel in her mouth while she was laughing so hard. His glare didn't help. But finally, she got the damn thing in, adjusted her mask strap and stood up.

He followed her example, but not well.

She sighed, then took hers out. "Just pretend you're a boxer and that's your mouth guard. Only it lets you breathe."

He put the mouthpiece all the way in.

"Good. Now, I like to let a little bit of water into the mask—not much, just a little. It'll help defog the lens.

But if you get too much in, just come up so your head's above water, pull the lower edge away from your face and let the water drain out. Then make sure the strap hasn't slipped down."

He nodded.

"Oh, and remember. Think mermaid."

This time he gave her a thumbs-up.

Meg's heart went pitter-pat. This was cuteness to the nth degree, and she wished their lips were free for kissing.

They continued into the water, and when it was deep enough, she eased herself down until her head was halfway under. There wasn't much to see so close to shore, but through the mask, the sand was beautiful.

Turning her head slightly, she found Alex, and he was snorkeling like an old pro. No freaking out at all, which was excellent.

She swam toward the coral reef, moving her feet like a mermaid's tail. Alex trailed at first, jerking a bit in the water, but she knew he would get it.

Even before they got to the reef, they started seeing massive schools of brightly colored fish, all swimming in astonishing synchrony. Despite the fact that she'd researched the local fish on the Internet, she was completely unprepared for the beauty of the real deal.

It was like swimming in paradise. No sound except the echo of her own breathing, nothing in her field of vision but magnificent coral and brilliant creatures. It was just like *Finding Nemo,* and she found herself tugging Alex's arm and pointing at the bumpy orange frogfish and the long-spined squirrelfish with its huge eyes, the purple sea fan, and so many other stunning things she didn't recognize. It didn't matter, it was…

Alex reached over and took her hand in his. They swam like that, calm, smooth, together. Just the two of them.

It was…magic.

ALEX'S LIFE DIDN'T LEND itself to tanning. Or much of anything that required stretches of leisure. Meg seemed happy lying on her towel, her head cradled on her crossed arms, and even though he'd prefer to be indoors, he wouldn't disturb her for anything. So, he'd tan.

He closed his eyes and tried to think of only here, only now, so of course, all he could think about was what came next.

Hanover was only the tip of the iceberg. When Alex returned to D.C., it was going to be all sound and fury, at least for a while. Then…

What the hell was he going to do with his life? He'd spent so much time making the decision to leave, he hadn't thought out where he should go.

He looked at Meg. He'd talk to her. Get her advice. Even if she was a damn fool when it came to her own work, she could be objective about his.

He felt like a moron for not telling her about the book. About all of it. But the book—it wasn't real. Not yet. Sure, he'd done research, and he'd even put together a detailed synopsis. But he'd only written a couple of chapters, and he had no idea if it was any good. His ego was large enough to make him think it didn't suck, but that wasn't something he could count on. It might suck. He didn't want to know.

If it did, if he couldn't write anything but political columns, then what? Take up flower arranging? Sell life insurance?

He could teach, but that had zero appeal. The trouble was he was good as a columnist. If only the price hadn't been so high.

"Hey."

He turned to find Meg staring at him. "What?"

"That sigh," she said.

"Sigh?"

"You just sighed like you found out Santa wasn't real."

He rose on his elbows. "What? He's not real?"

She smiled, but she wasn't gonna let it go. He could tell, because she took off her sunglasses. "What's going on?"

"Too much thinking," he said.

"About?"

"The meaning of life," he answered cryptically.

"It's 42. Next."

"Cute. Of course, I've read *The Hitchhiker's Guide to the Galaxy*, too."

"Seriously, spill. Pretend you're typing and tell me," she ordered.

"Are you sure? It's not pretty," he warned.

"That's okay. You are. And I'm a tough broad. So hit me with it. I can take it."

"I don't know what I want to be when I grow up," he said.

"What about what your parents suggested? Being a reporter in Europe?"

"That's their dream, not mine."

She rolled over, moved closer. Kept her sunglasses off. "What's yours? The book?"

"It could be. But I'm too much of a chicken to talk about it, let alone give it to someone to read."

"You already know you can write," she argued.

"Not fiction, I don't." Alex grimaced.

"Well, have you thought about writing something else? Not giving up the fiction, but taking what you've learned about politics and writing about that?" she suggested.

"Nonfiction?"

"Yeah. In addition to, not instead of. I mean writing something about what you've learned. How it's changed you. Why you've become so disillusioned."

"I'm not disillusioned. Just honest. Once you've seen the game, there's no going back."

"What would need to change to make it like you want it to be?" she asked.

"On the Hill?"

She nodded.

"Jeez, you have a month? A shake-up from the ground up, and even then, who the hell would listen?"

"I would," she said.

"That's nice. I know you would. But no one else wants to hear my musings on why the republic has gone into the toilet," he said sighing.

"Has it? Completely?" she asked.

"Not completely, no. But we're a greedy people who have no long-term vision."

"Are you afraid to write something like that?"

"Hell, yes," he said.

"Why?"

"Public ridicule. Never have liked it much." He rolled his eyes.

"That's it? What other people would think of you? Come on, Alex. I've read your column. You're not a wuss. You tell the truth, you don't back down. The politicians listen to you."

He smiled. "You're adorable."

"Flattery will get you laid, but it won't make me stop pushing."

"Ah. Thanks for the clarification. If I flatter you some more can we test the theory?"

"Nope. Well, yeah, but not right this minute," she said.

"Hey, I've got it. Let's both quit. Just walk away. Move to, I don't know, Idaho or Colorado. I'll write my book, you work part time at an animal hospital. One where you get to go home at five," he said.

Meg opened her mouth, but didn't say anything. She simply looked at him with an odd expression on her face. He expected her to laugh. She didn't.

15

"AREN'T WE SUPPOSED TO BE doing something?"

Alex turned his head toward her, putting his hand up to block the sun. "I have no idea."

"Damn," Meg said, "I left the schedule in the room. Don't remember much of it."

"Want me to go get it?"

"No," she said as she sat up, her skin warm, her hair almost dry. It wouldn't have bothered her to stay on the beach and vegetate, but there were too many people bringing too much noise with them. She didn't want to hear dueling boom boxes. She wanted peace and quiet and Alex. "How do you feel about going to the hotel?"

"Whatever you'd like."

"Come on, don't say that. What do you want to do?" she asked.

"I want to be with you and I don't much care where that happens," he stated.

She grinned. Ran her hand down her thigh, remembering his touch, the way his large hands made her feel very small. "Let's do it. We can get a copy of our schedule and see if we want to do any of it."

"Good plan." As he stood up, he raked a hand through his hair, making it stick up in just the right places. Gathering up his towel, he looked around, evidently trying to find a clear space to shake out the sand, but he was surrounded. With a shrug, he folded the thing and stuck it under his arm. When he glanced back at her, he seemed surprised. "What's that smile for?"

"Nothing in particular. I just think you're cute."

"Cute. First nice, now cute. Great."

She got up herself, debating whether she should put on her dress, but since everyone around her was fine with wearing bathing suits everywhere, she just folded it in with her towel. They walked to the end of the cove where they'd parked their cart. The sand had gotten warmer since they were there that morning, which meant they'd been at the cove for a while. It could have been an hour or three. It didn't matter. There was no place they had to be, even if they were signed up for something.

She was feeling quite languorous, and the idea of doing anything too physical didn't appeal. In fact, she kept thinking about the hammock by the bungalow. Maybe a cool drink. Some shade. Alex. Heaven.

Only heaven had to wait.

It was Tina. With Walter in tow. Both in beach gear, but Tina wore a big floppy hat.

"Hey, how are you two kids doing?" Alex asked. He gathered Meg close to him, arm around her waist.

Tina glanced at all the people on the beach, then back at Alex. "We're doing fine. Did you know there's someone looking for you?"

Alex's hand tightened. "A guy named Charlie Hanover?"

"He said he was a friend," Tina stated.

"I'll bet he did." Alex shook his head.

"Of course, we acted as if we didn't know a thing. I told Walter there was something fishy going on," Tina said, glancing at her husband.

Alex looked at Meg. "I guess I'm going to have to do something about him."

"It's still your vacation. I don't see why we have to give him the time of day," she said.

"I told you. He's relentless," Alex explained.

"Can we help?" Tina asked.

Alex smiled at her. "I appreciate the offer. I'm just not sure what's going to stop him."

"If you don't mind my asking, what does he want?" Tina asked.

"An interview. It's a long and dull story. If I was back in D.C., it wouldn't be a problem, but out here…"

"He was in his cart when he left, driving toward the boat dock. We're going back to the hotel, seeing as how Walter doesn't care for the crowds. But we'll be on the lookout for him, try to keep him away," Tina promised.

"He knows we're staying at the bungalow, so he's not going to go far," Alex said.

"Then let us go first. We'll distract him. Send him on a wild-goose chase." Tina's voice rose in her excitement, and her face glowed. It wasn't much, but she finally had something she could sink her teeth into. "Everyone deserves to be left in peace on their vacation."

Meg's gaze went from Tina to her husband. Walter was looking at her. It was, Meg thought, the first time he'd done that, at least when the four of them were together. And he was smiling.

"Thanks," Alex said. "But don't let it interfere with your own plans. Worse comes to worst, I'll talk to the guy."

"Not at our bungalows, you won't." Tina nodded once, as if she would brook no arguments.

Meg believed her. She gave Tina a hug before she took Alex's hand and they went to where they'd parked the cart.

She put her towel in the backseat, then climbed in next to him. He got the vehicle going, slowly though, since they had to watch for pedestrians, mopeds, bikes and other golf carts.

"Are you hungry yet?" he asked.

She shook her head. "Breakfast was huge. And wonderful."

Alex touched her leg. It was just a touch, nothing to get excited about, but that's just what happened. He touched her and her heart sped up, she stopped breathing, and when his hand lifted, she felt the loss.

She looked away, her pulse still racing, but for a completely different reason. God, she liked him. He was so much better in person, and he'd been terrific online. Leaving Escapades was going to hurt. Much worse than the little twinge at missing his touch. There was nothing in her real life that would make up for it, either. Just work.

She'd done it to herself, that much she knew. If she'd been stronger, if she hadn't felt so responsible for her clients, she could have had a rich life. There were a million things to do where she lived, a million people to get to know. Adult education, local gyms, groups of every kind. She used to belong to a professional organization that had pretty nifty monthly meetings, but after missing so many, she'd let her membership lapse.

She still had her girlfriends, but even those relationships were suffering. It wasn't that she didn't adore Becky and Debbi, she was just so damn tired all the time.

It was no way to live, and she had to do something about it. Period. No more screwing around. If the people on the mountain didn't like it, well, too bad. There were other vets, good ones. Alex was right. She was tired of being at their mercy.

When he'd made that joke about them running off together, it had hit her hard. What she'd been missing out on. The feelings she'd convinced herself she didn't have.

She looked at him again, at his strong profile. At his dark hair blowing in the breeze. The slight unconscious smile curving his lips.

What would it be like to be with him? Not for a few days, but for real? For keeps? What would it be like to wake up to him every morning? Sleep with him every night?

Longing gripped her, and the harder she tried to shake it, the deeper it ran. Things had changed for her since she'd first met Alex. Even though it was online, it was as real as it gets. She'd let him into her life. Given him an all-access pass. Last night, she'd given him the map to her body, and wouldn't you know it? He already knew the way.

"Meg?"

She turned to him, pasting on a smile. "Yeah?"

"Did you bring a camera?" he asked.

"Yes, I did," she answered.

"So did I."

"Why haven't we taken any pictures, then?" Meg wondered.

"I was just pondering that. I want to have pictures."

"Me, too."

"We'll have to get them as soon as we can. I don't want any more time to go by without a record," he said.

She touched his hand. "A record?"

"I want to remember all of this. Everything," he explained.

"I'm not going to take *those* kinds of pictures, you know," Meg said.

"Chicken," Alex teased.

"You betcha."

He slowed for another cart, then sped up as they approached the hotel entrance. After a few moments searching for an empty spot to park, they got out and went inside.

It felt perfectly natural to drift together, for their hands to meet. As if it was second nature. They fit. Which was wonderful. And a little sad.

They climbed the stairs, passed the fountain and entered the lobby. It was the least crowded place they'd been all day, but still there were folks. Couples. All of them cocooned in a haze of happy bliss. All of them touching, whether it was hands, or bumping hips, or arms around waists and shoulders. It was in the very air, pheromones being stirred by the big plantation fans.

At the activities desk, they got a copy of the schedule. It turned out to be just a little after ten, and they were up for the rock wall at ten thirty.

Alex tried to make Meg believe he was excited about it, but she could tell he wasn't enthused. At two, they were scheduled for the Jet Skis, which really did sound like fun. She'd never done that before, and she'd always wanted to.

She made her decision, and went back to the concierge. "We won't be rock climbing at ten thirty," she said. "So if someone else wants our spot, that's fine."

"Would you like to reschedule?" the woman asked.

Meg shook her head. "No, thanks."

When she turned to Alex, he seemed troubled. "You sure?" he pressed.

She nodded. "One thing first, then let's go back to the bungalow."

He cheered right up. "I'll sign up for that. Now, what's that first thing?"

"Waterfall," she said firmly.

"Ah, yes. Waterfall."

She took his hand and they walked toward the side exit to the big pool.

"So here's my question," Alex said, moving closer, his voice low so only she could hear. "Do you think there was anyone at all on this entire island that didn't have sex last night?"

She laughed. "I was just thinking that."

"Oh?"

"It's the island. I told you. Magic," she whispered.

He slowed. "You think?"

"You don't?"

He didn't answer.

THE LONGER CHARLIE WAITED, the more he wanted to pin Alex Rosten to the wall. He'd finally found out that Rosten was staying in the bungalows, not the hotel, but he still wasn't sure which bungalow. So he'd been driving in a circuit between all twelve of them, stopping anyone he could to ask. But no one seemed to know anything about Rosten or the woman he was shacking up with.

He'd called his editor, who'd told him the heat was on and that he'd better get the damn interview pronto, because every news organization in the country was on the trail. No way was Charlie going to miss out on being first.

He took a drink of tepid water from his bottle, wondering whether room service would deliver to a glorified golf cart. He hadn't remembered to bring any sunscreen, so he was turning into a goddamn tomato as he drove in his little circles.

When he did finally hear another cart coming down the path, he was more than ready. He had his tape recorder in his shirt pocket, his notepad on the seat next to him.

He spun the cart around and slammed on the brake. *Shit.* It was that older couple. They'd been useless before, and he doubted they'd be better now.

"Hello! Mr. Hanover!" the woman called out.

He sighed, but he waited. Maybe they knew something. But he wouldn't bet on it.

They drove up, the woman still waving, the man looking at him as if he wanted to sell him some insurance. "Mr. Hanover. Hello. Any luck?" the woman asked.

"No, no luck."

Their carts were parked too close together, and even though they were in the middle of a big expanse of sand and grass, he felt hemmed in.

"Well, we didn't actually see Alex…" she said.

He waited for the rest of the sentence. And waited. "Yes?"

The woman looked at her husband, then back at him. She pushed back her big hat, revealing a strip of pale skin. "We did happen to see his name on a list."

"A list?"

She nodded, turned to hubby once more. "Didn't we, Walter?"

"Yep. His name. On a list," Walter said.

"What list?"

"It was for the spa," she said.

"Oh?"

"It was a massage, I believe."

Her husband lifted his hand. "No, no, Tina, I think you're mistaken. It wasn't a massage at all."

"No?" She turned to him again. "Are you sure? Because I thought it was a massage."

"I think it was for something else. Some kind of hydrotherapy. Not sure what it's supposed to do for a body, but it was his name, all right," he insisted.

"But that wasn't the same list, Walter. That was the second list," she said.

"Second?" he echoed.

"There were two. Don't you remember? They were right there on the clipboards. Sitting on that beautiful marble desk," she said.

Charlie closed his eyes and cursed the day he was born. He listened to them jabber on until he couldn't take another second of it. "Hey!"

Tina and Walter turned to him, blinking.

"Did any of these appointments have times on them?" Charlie demanded impatiently.

"Why, yes," Tina said. "Alex should be there right now."

"Thank you." Charlie backed up his cart at the same time Walter got his in gear. Only, when Charlie started forward, so did Walter. Right into the side of Charlie's cart.

THE POOL WASN'T as crowded as the beach. In fact, one of the attendants put two lounges together for them, right near the deep end, and signaled the cocktail waitress. Alex settled down, watching Meg as she stared at the waterfall. She only looked away when it was time to order drinks. They both asked for a Bloody Mary, and they both wanted them weak.

He waited until they were alone, and turned to Meg. "What's the deal with the waterfall?"

"Oh, I just love them," she said, sighing.

"No story?" he asked.

She shook her head, but if he wasn't mistaken, her cheeks got a little pink. "It's stupid."

"Come on. I'll never tell."

"*Last of the Mohicans*," she said.

"The book?" he asked, confused.

"No, the movie. Daniel Day Lewis. Madeleine Stowe. The score. The waterfall. I swooned."

"Swooned? Really?"

"If you must know, yes. Really. I didn't actually fall to the ground or anything, but yes, swooning occurred. So now you know my secret. It goes with you to the grave."

He crossed his heart. "They can torture me. Not too much, mind you, because I hate pain, but they can pinch me from now until tonight, and I won't say one word."

She laughed, and he wanted her. Now. Under the damn waterfall. He looked at it, but there didn't seem to be enough privacy for his diabolical plan, and he had no intention of getting kicked out. At least they could kiss. Maybe do a little fondling. Fondling was good.

"Shall we?" she asked. "Swim?"

He nodded. As he was lifting his hands to dive into the pool, she pinched his ass.

"Hey," he protested.

"Just testing that theory," she said.

"Do it again, and I sing like a bird, honey."

She shoved him in.

He sputtered as he came up in the cool water, determined that the assault would not go unavenged. Worse, she was standing at the edge, laughing. Laughing!

Swimming toward her, he thought about grabbing her ankle, but that seemed foolhardy. And too direct. He needed to get her back when she least expected it. "You gonna stand up there all morning?"

She shook her head, then dived over his head. She was no Louganis, but the dive succeeded well enough. And when she came up for air, with her hair all sleek and dark, her eyelashes pearled with water, her lips parted showing just a hint of teeth, he figured he'd give her ten minutes by the damn waterfall and then they were going to the bungalow.

"Hey, you look pretty good wet," Meg said, swimming into him with such fervor his back smacked against the side of the pool.

"What is it with you? Do you take delight in hurting me? You're the one who likes that kind of thing, not me."

She pushed herself against him, her pelvis to his. "Oh, I think I could show you a thing or two. Make you beg for mercy."

"Oh, really?"

She nodded, her upper teeth biting her lower lip. And her hand slipped into his trunks. The front of his trunks.

He panicked. Grabbed her wrist and pulled her free, then swam away as fast as he could. Hadn't the woman ever heard of shrinkage?

By the time she caught up with him, they were at the waterfall. She grinned like a loon. But as she approached him, she gave him a pathetic attempt at a frown. "I'm sorry, Alex. Did I scare you?"

"You're asking for it, woman."

"Asking for what?"

He grabbed her arm and pulled her against his body. Her mouth opened in surprise and he took full advantage, kissing her hard. It wasn't easy treading water, but he managed to keep them from drowning. When he finally let her go, she sank. But only for a minute. When she came up, she swam past him to the waterfall, ducked under it, swam behind it, held her hands out to feel it, swam back under it, yelled, "You stay alive, no matter what occurs! I will find you. No matter how long it takes, no matter how far, I will find you!" Then she swam back to him, and when she was in the exact position she'd been in two minutes before, she smiled. "Bungalow?"

MEG CARRIED THE DRINKS up the stairs while Alex got the towels from the back of the cart. The table had been cleared from breakfast, the drapes had all been opened and the bed was made, the netting flapping gently in the breeze. She took a sip of her Bloody Mary, put both glasses down on the table, and went for the bathroom, feeling guilty she was leaving a trail of sand.

She heard Alex behind her, and that was very good, because in a few seconds she wanted him naked and in the shower. With her, of course.

Briefly, she thought about the hammock idea, and decided they could do that after.

She stripped so quickly he hadn't even reached the bathroom door yet. When he arrived, he looked pleased with her outfit.

It didn't take him long to peel his trunks off, and gosh, he seemed very enthusiastic.

As she turned on the shower he moved right in behind her. His hands went to her waist, his thighs pressed against hers and without any warning at all, his cock, quite thick and very warm, slipped between the cheeks of her ass.

As the water got warmer, so did she. Alex rocked gently up and down, sliding against her right there, and she forgot how to breathe, it was so incredibly hot.

He held her steady, not letting her stand straight, not letting her move at all. It was his show all the way.

She couldn't help but wonder what he planned to do from there. There were several different options, and she wasn't capable of choosing. Every place their bodies connected was an erogenous zone, including the little space on the back of her hips where his thumbs rubbed in short strokes.

But it was what he was doing to her behind that had her losing her mind. It was a totally new feeling, one she'd never guessed could be so thrilling. Just rubbing. Nothing more. But oh, God, it made every nerve ending buzz.

He leaned over her, and she felt his weight on her back, his breath on her neck. "Is it hot yet?"

"Yeah, I am."

He chuckled. "I was talking about the water."

"Screw the water."

"Oh, no, babe. I'm going to screw you." He licked her neck, a long wet slide of tongue on flesh, only stopping when he reached her ear. He captured the lobe between his teeth and bit her. Her knees buckled. If he hadn't been holding her up, she'd have fallen.

He leaned back, bringing her with him. "I think it's your turn, don't you?"

"What?" she asked, hardly recognizing her own voice.

"Yesterday, I washed you. How about you wash me?"

She nodded, felt his hands slip away. Stepping into the shower, she reached for the sponge. He joined her as she squeezed out a whole bunch of liquid soap. His hand ran up her back, making her shiver, and then it was gone. When she turned, he was standing directly beneath the showerhead. The water poured over his closed eyes, his lips, his chin. She followed the path to his chest, its sparse hair matted, down to the hollow of his stomach and over his rigid cock.

Moving in front of him, she raised the sponge to his broad chest, and taking her cue from him, remembering how it had felt, she painted circles of slick soap, following each turn with the palm of her hand.

He opened his eyes, and she stared into them as she continued to wash him, loving the feel of his muscles, of all the places he was firm and strong.

Her hands moved down, washing him carefully, not missing a thing. She noticed, by feel alone, that his respiration quickened, that despite his stony expression, his seeming implacability, he felt it all.

Lower still, she wondered when he'd break. When she brushed the back of her hand over the tip of his cock? When she grasped his length with the sponge and squeezed? Or when she cupped his balls with her palm and rolled them in her fingers?

That was it. That moment.

His hands grasped her upper arms tightly, and he lifted her up off her feet until her lips touched his. He devoured her mouth, thrusting with his tongue, in and out, mimicking what they were going to do, stealing her breath.

When her feet touched the shower floor again, he turned her around and pushed her against the back of the stall. He found her hands and brought them up above her head.

"Don't move," he said, his voice nearly a growl.

He kicked her feet apart, and then he gripped her waist once more. He pulled back, making her spine bow, her ass stick out.

Then he let go with his right hand, and she felt fingers enter her, pushing into a wet heat that had nothing to do with the shower.

"So hot," he said, "so ready."

She laid her cheek on the cool tile, her hands tightening into fists as she waited for the fingers to pull away. She didn't have to wait long.

He entered her all at once, filling her completely. Her head flew back as she cried out with the brute force.

He had her by the waist again, holding her steady as he thrust, withdrew almost all the way, then thrust once more. But that wasn't enough for him. He pulled her back as he pushed forward, his hips slapping her ass almost as hard as his hand had the night before.

It was unbelievable, the power of his thrusts, the intensity of his every move. She braced her arms so she wouldn't bang her head, so she wouldn't slip, but he held her so firmly she couldn't have fallen.

"So good," he said, that low, low voice winding its sinuous way inside her. "So beautiful. God, you make me crazy."

She opened her mouth, but all that came out were gasps as he continued to turn her into a quivering mass of need. He never let up, never varied his ruthless rhythm, not even when he took her right wrist in his hand and pulled her arm down.

Confused, she struggled for a moment, but then he brought her hand between her legs. He thrust into her, stopped, leaned over so his mouth was close to her ear. "Do it. Come for me."

He let her go, and she obeyed, bringing her finger to

her aroused clitoris. His hands were on her waist again, and she had to follow the back-and-forth, the pounding heat that thrilled her more than she could have ever imagined.

She rubbed with her fingers, but it didn't take much. She felt it rising, squeezed him hard as her muscles tensed.

He moaned, and for the first time, he lost the pace. His movements became erratic, and his hands on her waist tightened.

She came so hard her ears rang and her vision blackened. She had to brace herself against the wall because a second later, he lifted her feet off the ground as he came, his howl echoing off the walls.

She hung there, trembling, spasms rolling through her whole body. And when she touched ground, he slumped over her back, panting against her neck.

"Holy shit," she whispered.

He smiled against her skin. "Oh, yeah."

16

MEG COULDN'T MOVE. NOT AN inch. She wasn't just worn out from the most intense sexual experience of her life, she was spinning from the fact that the man who'd just turned her inside out was the same man who made her laugh, loved old jazz and remembered her charm bracelet.

So she just leaned against the shower stall, waiting to see if her heart would ever stop pounding, if this would all turn out to be an insanely wonderful dream.

His touch surprised her, but it was very gentle. Oddly, it was on her head. Ah. Shampoo. Oh, God, he was shampooing her hair.

Second favorite scene, right after the waterfall in *Mohicans*? When Robert Redford washed Meryl Streep's hair in *Out of Africa*. Two in one day was way outside the box. This was the stuff of magic, of fairy tales. And yet Alex's hands, firm and sudsy, massaged her tenderly. Right here, right now. Freeze frame, please. Whoever was in charge of moments, she wanted this one to last forever. Well, this one would have to include the last twenty minutes, too, right? Because she wouldn't be this wasted if he hadn't taken her to a place way past anything she'd ever imagined sex was.

She sighed, letting the shivers take her. Breathing in the scent of coconut. Knowing she was in deep, deep trouble.

ALEX GOT THEM BOTH rinsed, turned the water off and bundled Meg into a towel. His own legs weren't as steady as they could be, but she was in worse shape. He helped her to the big bed where she crashed, flinging her arms above her head.

She opened one eye. "Thirsty."

"Bloody Mary? Or soda?"

"Soda."

He went to the minibar, which they hadn't even looked in yet. It was wonderfully stocked, with everything from chocolate bars to wine. But there was plenty of soda, and he picked out a diet for her, a full-octane for himself.

He popped her top, put it by her night table, then climbed over her limp, perfect body, and sighed as he fell back to join her.

"Alex?"

"Yeah?"

"Where did that come from?" she whispered.

"I don't know," he said.

Her hand flopped onto his stomach. "Wow."

"Uh-huh."

She turned her head. "That ever happen to you before?"

"Nope," he said.

"Wow," she repeated.

"It was you," he said.

"I doubt it. From what I can remember, I just hung on for dear life," she said.

He turned to face her. "No. I mean it was *you.*"

She blinked. Her lips parted. "Oh."

He smiled as the truth of it came home. It was her. He'd never wanted to possess a woman more than he did Meg. Even now, when he was still trying to regulate his heart rate, he wanted her again.

The setting couldn't have been more perfect. Everything he could have dreamed up to impress her, to take her breath away. But it wasn't the island. The magic here was what was happening between them.

He'd expected...fun. A break. Someone he could talk to. He'd expected to get lucky. To forget about the rest of the world and just relax.

He hadn't expected Meg.

Whatever had happened in that shower, it wasn't just sex. Okay, yeah, it was the most unbelievably fantastic sex he'd ever experienced in his life, but it wasn't because he'd suddenly become Mr. Studmuffin. He rarely kidded himself about his prowess. He was fine in the sack, and he'd had no complaints. When he was younger, his stamina had been pretty damn astonishing. Then he'd learned, from some pretty terrific women, that a woman needs a lot more than stamina.

He'd always tried to give his best, but until today, he hadn't gotten it. Sex, when it was right, was completely, utterly, only about her.

Why didn't he know this? No one had told him. He'd never read about it. This was completely new information. Vital information.

The only problem with this startling discovery was its limited use.

Three more days, and once again they'd be thousands of miles apart.

The only possible solution was to fix that. Maybe they couldn't be in the same state, but there were planes. Lots of planes. Lots of places they could meet. It wouldn't be easy, but hell, they could do it. Once a quarter. That was doable. It would do them both a world of good. He'd just have to convince her of the brilliance of his plan.

"Alex?"

"Yes?" he said.

"We didn't use a condom."

"Oh, shit."

"Which is semi-okay, 'cause I'm on the pill," she said.

"Well, you don't have to worry about any of the other stuff on my end," he said.

"Me, either. Phew. And Alex? Why is the phone blinking red?"

He lifted up on his elbows and looked at the telephone. It was connected only to the hotel. "Maybe it's about the Jet Ski thing?"

"Suppose I should find out?" she murmured.

"The phone's all the way over there," he said.

"I know," she said. "But I have to sit up if I want to drink the soda. If I'm sitting up already, it shouldn't be that hard to walk over to the phone."

"That's ambitious."

"I'm one tough broad."

"I'll say."

He turned just enough so that he could see her as she struggled up. As she tipped the soda back. As she tucked the towel around herself and walked to the phone and pressed 0.

"Hi, this is Meg Becker from the bungalow."

She picked up the phone and brought it back to the bed. She smiled at Alex, then turned quickly. "Yes? Oh, okay. No, I know the number, thank you. Um, is the nearest phone in the hotel?"

Alex sat up. In the space of those few words, Meg had changed. Her expression had gone from relaxed bliss to tight concern. Her shoulders hunched, and when she turned back to look at him, there was a sadness that had no business being there.

"Thank you," she said again, then she hung up the phone.

"What's happened?" he asked.

"I have to go to the hotel," she said.

"Meg, what is it?"

"Pippin's dying."

"Pippin?"

She nodded. "He's a horse. A really wonderful horse. He's old, and he's stopped eating."

"A horse?"

"I know it's hard to understand. You'd think it wouldn't matter, but if you knew this horse…I was there when he was born, you know. I was a kid, and my dad took me along with him to the Kellers'. It was late, like two in the morning, but he got me out of bed so I could help. I didn't do much except get in the way, but it was the first time I'd seen a horse foal."

"So he's a friend."

She sniffed, and her eyes glistened. "The woman who owns him has a daughter with rheumatoid arthritis. She has trouble with her hands, with her knees. But she rides him every day. He's kept her going since she was old enough to walk. All these years he's taken care of her with such patience and grace. I have to call, Alex. I have to make sure she's all right."

Meg stood to head for the dresser.

"Wait. I have a phone." He got up and went to his suitcase. The cell phone was in a side pocket.

"You cheated," she said.

"It was only in case of emergency, and I think this qualifies."

She joined him, took the phone and kissed him. It was nothing like the kisses in the shower. That he could give her this little thing, this cell phone, made him unreasonably happy.

She went back to the bed and sat cross-legged, sweetly vulnerable in her white towel. He heard the beep of the phone waking up as he pulled some boxers out of his drawer. Once he had those on, he sat next to her.

"Missy? It's Doc."

Her voice was different. It was deeper, more compassionate. No wonder they wanted to keep her all to themselves.

"Missy, honey, wait. Take a breath, okay? Just breathe for a minute. Now, sweetie, I can't come back today. I wish I could be there with you, but you're going to get through this, okay? Missy?"

He lay down as silently as he could, not wanting to interfere. A nap would have been nice, but not while she was in the middle of all of this.

So he just looked at her. The shape of her nose entranced him. The urge to touch it was strong.

"Honey, Dr. Scott is a wonderful man, and he's going to make sure Pippin doesn't suffer at all, okay? But Missy, the real job, the important job, is yours. Not mine or Dr. Scott's. Honey, you need to go be with Pippin. You need to touch him, and pet him, and tell him what a wonderful friend he's been. How much he's meant to you. And you need to let him know that it's okay to go now. He's worked hard for many years, and now he needs to rest, but he won't rest until he knows you're going to be okay without him."

Meg lowered her head as she listened, and Alex could feel how this conversation was hurting her. But her voice didn't reveal it at all. Her feeling for this girl ran deep, and Alex couldn't help but regret his cavalier attitude toward the people on the mountain.

It still wasn't healthy to give so much. He wondered if she was even capable of giving one iota less.

"I know, Missy. I remember. Pippin's the best friend ever. Now you go on, and be with him. He needs you. You make sure he knows you're going to be fine, okay? Because you are. You're so strong, Missy. You can do this."

Alex got up, went back to his suitcase and pulled one of his cards out of the same pocket where he kept the phone. He slipped it onto the bed in front of Meg.

She looked up at him, eyes red with tears, questioning. But when she glanced at the card again, she nodded.

He went back to his place and Meg said goodbye to Missy, after giving her the cell phone number and telling her she could call anytime.

When she hung up, Meg immediately phoned out again, to Dr. Scott, who was already on his way to the Kellers'. The conversation was brief, and once it was over, she closed the phone and lay down, curling into Alex's side.

He put his arm around her and held her for a long time. If she cried, it was very quiet—only a sniffle once or twice. But she held on to him as if he brought her comfort.

He tried to remember the last time he'd done that for anyone. Not Ellen. She'd never needed him. Never turned to him for anything, let alone comfort.

Brushing his hand over Meg's arm, Alex closed his eyes and thought about a lot of things. Mostly about choices. So many behind him, all of them leading to this moment. With this woman who cared so much about the people in her life that she wept for the passing of a horse.

MEG SCRUNCHED UP closer to Alex and put her hand on his chest. Right above his heart. She breathed through her mouth as quietly as she could, focusing on finding his heartbeat. There it was. Steady, strong. Like Alex himself.

She hated disappointing him. And he would be when he found her back on her mountain, same hours, same demands. All that talk about making a change. How? Who was she going to stop seeing? Alfred, with his five dogs, all of them old and hanging on out of sheer determination? Janice and Bob and their menagerie, most of them with allergies, most of them so skittish she couldn't get a single one into the office? The Johnsons' alpacas? The grade school?

She felt terrible that Missy and Pippin had to go through this alone. Before Meg left, she'd known that Pippin was going downhill. Why hadn't she made time to talk to Missy, to prepare her for this? It had been her own selfishness, nothing else. She'd spent the time buying expensive tiny dresses and getting her Brazilian wax.

"Alex?"

"Yeah, honey?"

Honey. Oh, God. That shouldn't have felt this good. "Meg?"

"I just wanted to say thank-you," she whispered.

"For what?"

"This is the best present I've ever had. I still can't believe you did it."

"Why wouldn't you believe it? I've become quite fond of you, Ms. Becker."

"Odd, isn't it? How easy it was to talk when we'd never met," she murmured.

"It's easy now. Isn't it?"

"Yes. Definitely. You're better than ever. I just hope that when we get back, it won't, you know, change."

He squeezed her arm. "You don't think it'll be different?"

She looked up at him. To his dark eyes, and his wonderful lower lip. "Different isn't always better."

"What are you asking me?"

"I'm not sure. I guess I need to know that you'll still be there. That we're still going to type," she said.

"Of course we are. Why in hell wouldn't we?" he asked.

"Please don't be upset," she said.

"I'm not," he stated.

"You sound like you are," she told him.

He sat up, dislodging her so he could turn to face her. "What's this about? You think I brought you here so I could end our relationship?"

"Relationship? Is that what we have?" she queried.

"I guess. What would you call it when a person can't wait to get home so he can log in? I check for you every night. You know that, don't you?" he asked.

"And I check for you, whenever I can. When you're there, I'm so glad," she said.

"But now?"

"Nothing. Never mind. It was silly," she said.

"Talk to me," he ordered.

"I should go back."

"I see."

She climbed off the bed, suddenly uncomfortable in just the towel. Tugging open a drawer, she pulled out a pair of shorts, panties, bra and a tank top, then went into the bathroom. She almost closed the door, but felt weird about it, so she just put on the clothes as quickly as she could. When she saw her hair, she shuddered. It was going to be hell brushing it out.

She took a deep breath and went back into the room, stopping before she hit the corner of the bed. "I can't leave them. They count on me. It's complicated."

He nodded. "Okay. That makes sense. You have a relationship with these people. You've been with them a long time."

"That's right. I have. I understand what's going on with them," she said.

"That's important. Continuity can make things easier for everyone," he said.

"Continuity. That's right. That's exactly right."

"It's funny," he said. "I've been thinking a lot about that. I really did have it made at the *Post*. I worked long and hard to get all my sources. Now, all that's gone."

"Are you sorry?" she asked.

"Sad. But not sorry."

He got up, padded across the wood floor, and for the first time she really noticed his boxers. The pattern that she'd thought was abstract wasn't. It was tiny pictures of the characters from *The Simpsons*. Marge, Homer, Bart, Apu. "Nice shorts."

"Mmm," he said. "Shorts."

She laughed, because he really did sound like Homer. "You know, that's what really got to me."

"What?"

"Aside from all that music stuff. You got my references."

"They were quite subtle, too. Let's see," he said, "'Eat my shorts.' 'Mmm, doughnuts.' I had to be on my toes."

"You were. It was pretty cool."

"It was. It is," he told her.

"So, that's all I'm saying. When we get back, it'll be the same. Only we'll have this, too."

"Works for me," he agreed.

"Great."

"Can I just say that you were amazing on the phone?

Missy's gonna be fine. You were perfect, all the way from here," he said.

Meg's eyes welled up again, and she wiped them, not wanting to cry. She'd been so determined to change things. But some things couldn't be changed. Not without hurting a whole lot of people.

"You know what?"

"Hmm?"

He brushed her arm with the back of his hand. "There's a hammock out there with our names written all over it. And you know what else?"

"What?"

"If we call now, they'll bring us anything we want. Hammock service, I believe they call it. I was thinking about drinks. Something with umbrellas. And perhaps some lunch. Something that's easy to eat when we're swaying in the breeze. What do you think?"

"I think it sounds wonderful," she said.

"Any preferences?" he asked.

"You order. You did a great job with breakfast."

He kissed her very gently on the lips, then on the forehead. "I'm glad I've got you in my corner, Meg."

He went to the phone, and she stepped outside. All she wanted was to shut down. To stop thinking, stop worrying. She couldn't do anything more for Missy. It was out of her hands. What she could do was be here, be with Alex. Let it go, at least for the next few days.

If nothing else, she could have this, right?

17

THE HAMMOCK WAS MADE OF rope, hanging in between two huge palm trees. There was a large pillow at the top, and a little table within easy reach on the right. The view from the hammock was straight out of the heart of paradise. The sea, aquamarine and so clear you could see all the way down to your toes. The sky, bluer than anything over Los Angeles, with clouds made of cotton and angels' wings.

Nothing was going to interfere with the perfection of this moment. Hearing Alex walking down the stairs from the bungalow to the sand filled her with a giddy anticipation. She backed up to the edge of the hammock, braced her arms, and slid onto ropes that were surprisingly comfy.

She looked over to see Alex smiling. He'd changed from his boxers to another pair of blue trunks. Did he own any other color? She'd have to find out. It was a good project, something she could totally delve into.

"What are you grinning at?" he asked.

"Laughing in anticipation," she replied.

"Ah, good." He walked around the palm tree so he could get to his side of the hammock. "You made this look easy."

"This thing is the size of a small country. You shouldn't have any trouble," she joked.

"We'll see," he said, and used her exact approach to climb aboard. A few seconds later he was lying next to her, his side pressing against hers, their heads sharing the big pillow.

He slipped his arm under her neck, and Meg adjusted her body so she was curled into him.

"Feeling better?"

She nodded, rubbing her cheek on his chest. "Much. I've wanted to be in this hammock since I saw it on the brochure."

"It's pretty spectacular."

"Who'd have thought rope could feel so good?" she murmured.

Alex let his fingers drift over her arm. "Oh, I can think of a whole bunch of naughty answers to that question. How can I pick just one?"

"I'm too blissed out to pinch you," she retorted.

"I'll consider myself pinched, how's that?"

She looked up with a grin. "Excellent, thank you."

They lay there for several minutes, the breeze fanning them but not moving the hammock. The clouds drifted silently above and the sea lapped at the shore like a cat drinking warm milk.

"Alex?"

"Hmm?"

"What are you going to do?"

"Imagine all the different ways I can make you shiver."

"Oh," she said, liking the sound of that. "But, no, I mean when you get back."

"Ah."

"I know you've been thinking about it." She ran her hand over his belly, sighing as his muscles tensed and relaxed.

"That's true. Which I realize is against the rules, but I've always been a rebel," he said.

"What have you come up with?"

"That my life, up till noon yesterday, was not everything I'd hoped it would be."

"Boy, you have been thinking."

"My curse," he said as he stroked her shoulder.

"You're trying to sidetrack me."

"Are you sure you want to talk about this?" He moved his hand up, brushing his fingers softly over her chin.

"Yes," she said, determined not to get distracted. Yet.

"Okay. Don't say I didn't warn you."

She looked up at him, so she could watch his eyes.

He met her gaze squarely. "I'm done with the paper."

Her mouth opened to protest, but she bit the words back. She wanted to hear all of what he said, what he felt. "Go on."

"It's going to happen. It's already happened. It doesn't matter. It was sucking the life out of me. The thought of going back to that grind makes me ill. I just can't do it anymore."

"So you're going to write your novel?"

"Yeah. And I've been thinking about what you suggested. I can do both. Work on the novel and write about the things I've learned in Washington. I have no idea if either will succeed, but I've got to try," he said.

"That's pretty major," she observed.

"It is. And all because of you."

"You keep saying that, but I don't understand how."

He looked at her for a long moment, letting his gaze linger on her eyes, her lips. "Because it was your birthday. And because I wanted to do something special for you. I took a damn big risk, asking you to meet me here. It could have turned out very differently."

"I'll say," she agreed dryly.

He cleared his throat and she wondered if they'd gotten a little too close for comfort. "What was your worst fear?" he asked, and sure enough, his voice had changed.

"That's easy. That you'd be this totally nice guy, with great intentions, and that you'd really like me."

He laughed. "I'm your worst fear?"

"No, the fear was that you'd be all those things, and I'd feel nothing." It was her turn for restlessness. She moved, sat up, curling her legs beneath her as the hammock swung. "Not even hate you, just feel no connection. And that we'd somehow get through the five days, and we'd go back home and it would never be the same again. I don't think you have any idea how important to me our talks are, Alex," she said.

"Yeah, I think I do."

"No. No, I can't even explain it to myself. It's not that I don't love my work. I do. There's nothing better than caring for animals. They're wonderful and they depend on me, and sometimes I can really help." She touched his arm, but she couldn't be still. She wanted to pace, but she didn't want to leave him. Instead, she focused on the ocean. Took a deep breath before she met his gaze once more. "But for the last few years, maybe longer, I haven't felt it. The joy. They don't understand that they're pulling on me. Not the animals, the people. Taking little pieces every day. They love their pets. Too much sometimes. It's an odd group of misfits on that mountain. It's become their place to hide. They're so proud of being separate."

She took his hand again, folding his fingers between her own. "Did you know most of the parents home-school their kids? Not for religious reasons, or even the sad state of the schools. They do it because it keeps them on the mountain."

"What do they want from you?" he asked.

"Comfort. Like you said. Continuity. You'd have to have known my father to really understand. He was a remarkable man. No one could have been more dedicated to his profession. He lived for work, and there was nothing more important."

"Not even his little girl?"

Meg closed her eyes. She pulled her free arm tight against her body. "That would be a no. He didn't spend a lot of time at home. Not in the home part, at least. He was always in the office, or out on a house call. He'd come in late, leave early. When he was home, he was asleep until the phone rang."

"How did your mother cope with that?" Alex asked.

"She adored him. The sun rose and set on his shoulders. She cooked, she cleaned, she made our clothes. I never saw her when she wasn't put together. Her hair was always neat, everything was ironed. A real Stepford Wife. When my father died, she fell completely apart.

She went to live with her sister, who was a nurse. She's on medication, and she will be for the rest of her life."

"I'm sorry."

"Me, too. Because my mother had this killer sense of humor. She was a riot. I think she could have done stand-up. Seriously, she was incredibly witty. Had a degree in English lit, but she never did anything with it," Meg said.

Alex sat up, although it wasn't the most graceful move ever. He ignored the swaying of the hammock as he got resettled. "But she didn't have a sense of humor about the housework, did she?"

"Oh, no. That was sacrosanct. Everything that touched my father was deadly serious."

"Is he why you went to veterinary school, or was she?"

Meg glanced up, prepared to see him smug, but he wasn't. His eyes were filled with compassion, and her heart lurched. "That's pretty observant for a columnist."

"It's always easier to see outside of ourselves," he said.

"I can't leave there," she repeated.

"Because…?"

"You heard that conversation. You know how they count on me."

"They'd survive," he insisted.

"You think it's that easy? Buh-bye, nice knowing you, here's the new doc?"

"Simple, yes," he said. "Easy, no."

"It's been my whole life," she told him.

He touched her cheek gently. "I understand that."

"I have no concept of anything else."

"I know that, too. But, Meg, don't you think you deserve to know more? To find out who you are? Not who your father wanted you to be. Or your mother. But who *you* want to be?"

"I'm not brave like you are," she said.

"I know that's not true. You came here, didn't you?"

She laughed. "To a fabulous tropical island? All expenses paid? Yeah, it was brutal."

"You didn't know me," he pointed out.

"Yes, I did. I do. I know you better than any other person in my life. Meeting you just confirmed it. Face it, Rosten, you're an open book."

He laughed then. "Jesus, if anyone I knew heard you say that, they'd think you were nuts. I'm the most closed son of a bitch I know. I don't open up to anyone."

"Except to Mountain Vet."

"She is the exception," he agreed.

"Why?" Meg asked.

"Why you, you mean?"

She nodded.

He let out a slow breath. "You made it safe. Not to mention fun. I know one trait you picked up from your mother."

"I make a mean tuna casserole?"

"Yep, that's the one," he exclaimed.

"Do you really see yourself as closed off? I find that so hard to believe," she said.

"I've lived in D.C. a long time. I believe about two percent of what I hear. I've trained myself—well, at least till yesterday—to never give a thing away, because there are very big, very dangerous sharks where I work. It wasn't a stretch, however. Remember, I come from the land of intellectual reason. Light reading in my house, and this was when I was a kid, mind you, was Nietzsche."

"You're kidding."

"Only slightly. My parents, unlike yours, had no sense of humor, at least about themselves. They believe in the law, in the constitution, in justice, which, by the way, they propound is a completely separate entity from the law," he said.

"But you're a riot."

He looked at her sharply. "A riot?"

"You make me laugh all the time. How is it possible that you can keep this huge part of you a secret? Surely you have someone close, someone who knows," she said.

His smile broke her heart, it was so sad. "Aren't we a special pair? I can't laugh, you can't say no." He stopped, blinked. "Hey, wait a minute."

"Ha-ha. You can't laugh, my ass."

"Your ass is nothing to laugh about."

"This is a serious discussion," she said, smacking him lightly.

"Too serious. We're on vacation," he insisted.

"But you still want me to quit, don't you?"

He reached over and pulled her close. She uncurled her legs, ready to lie down again, ready to be held tight.

"I want what would make you happy," Alex said. "You're young, you're gorgeous, you're bright. I could go on and on. And you're stuck up on a mountain with a bunch of llamas and borderline cult members. You do the math," he said deadpan.

"You're right. We are on vacation," she admitted.

"Speaking of which, where are our drinks?"

"They really deliver to a hammock?"

"They do indeed."

"What did you order?"

"For you? A totally girlie drink. Umbrellas, whirled in a blender, the whole nine yards," he confessed.

"And for you?"

"A Shirley Temple."

Meg giggled as he took his sweet time getting horizontal. It seemed impossible, but in the last hour she'd grown to like Alex even more. She'd also come to have great respect for his sexual prowess, but that wasn't the only reason for her raised esteem.

This was one hell of a man. He continued to surprise her. To delight her. And he lived a gazillion miles away. Which wasn't fair at all.

"Hey, what's that frown for?" he asked.

"Thoughts of home," she said.

"That's not allowed. However…"

"What?"

"I hear our drinks."

"They talk?" she teased.

"No, but the waiter drives a golf cart."

She sat up, with him pushing, and he sat up, with her pulling.

When she looked, she saw it wasn't a waiter at all. It was Walter and Tina, and Tina was waving like a madwoman. They drove up near the bungalow, then got out of the cart. To Meg's amazement, Walter took hold of Tina's hand as they walked toward the hammock. Both of them were smiling.

"It looks like you two have been having a wonderful time," Meg said.

"We have," Tina declared, her voice high and light, and years younger than just last night. "We've been playing with your friend Charlie."

Alex climbed down, making the hammock sway. "Explain playing, if you don't mind?"

Tina looked at Walter and they both laughed. It changed him completely. He actually had very nice eyes. "We found him here, stalking," she related. "And we played the dotty old couple, rambling on and on."

"She was the one," Walter said, looking as if he was enjoying the game. "She was so creative. I think she missed her calling."

"It was too much fun." Tina beamed at her husband. "He was simply fuming. And then—and this was all Walter—we hit his cart with ours."

"No!" Alex said, his own grin growing. "I bet he loved that."

"He was beside himself. By the time we got disentangled—"

"She got his key," Walter interjected. "I still don't know how."

"By that time, I thought we were going to have to call the paramedics," Tina said.

"Then?" Alex asked.

"Oh, he thinks you're either getting a massage or a hydrotherapy treatment at the spa. And he also thinks you moved out of the bungalows, back to the hotel," Tina said.

Alex turned to Meg, the expression on his face priceless.

"That's not the best part, though," Tina said, linking her arm with Walter's.

Meg got out of the hammock to stand by Alex. He pulled her close immediately, and she could tell he was enjoying this as much as the Lesters.

"It turns out," Walter said, "that we ran into a Mr. Castellano. Who, it also turns out, owns this resort."

"Lovely man. Great taste in art." Tina grinned at her husband once more before she turned back. "He bought us a drink, which was very nice, and we couldn't help it, we told him we think Mr. Hanover's a stalker."

Walter laughed. "I believe you used the words 'Peeping Tom.'"

"Walter, you haven't laughed like that in…" She turned back to Meg and Alex. "I might have said something about a Peeping Tom. Long story short, your Mr. Hanover will be leaving the island tonight."

"*What?*"

Meg laughed as she and Alex said the word at the same moment. "Butch is kicking Charlie out?" she asked.

Walter nodded. "Tonight."

Alex hugged Meg, then went over and hugged Tina. He opened his arms to Walter, who stuck out his hand, so they shook in a manly fashion. "This is great. Beyond great. I can't thank you enough."

Tina laughed. "We haven't had so much fun in ages. How we bamboozled that awful man! He really does like to curse, doesn't he?"

"He does. And I'm sure I'll hear all the best words as soon as I get back. But in the meantime, thank you. You really have saved our vacation," Alex said.

Just then, another cart appeared down the path, and happily, it wasn't the odious Charlie. It was their drinks.

"Join us?" Meg asked. "I'm sure the driver can be back in a flash with more."

"No, none for us," Tina said, stepping aside so the waiter could drive closer. "We've had a lot of excitement today, and we both need a nap."

"We owe you," Alex said. "Dinner. Before you leave."

Tina tugged on her husband's hand, leading him toward their bungalow. "It's a deal."

Walter caught up and kissed her on the temple.

Meg turned back to see the waiter had left them two piña coladas and a spectacular fruit plate that had not only the requisite pineapple, but chunks of fresh coconut, mangoes, papayas, and some fruit she couldn't identify. "Wow."

"I'll say. Good for them." Alex looked past her to where Tina and Walter had gone. "Good for us, too, but mostly, good for them."

She couldn't wait another second. She had to kiss him. So she did.

When they finally broke apart, it was time to nibble and sip and curl back into the hammock. For the first time since the phone call, Meg relaxed. The fruit and the drinks helped, but it was mostly because she'd come to a brand-spanking-new realization. As long as Alex was in her life, she had someone who was not only kind, but who got her. She could tell him anything, and while he might not agree with her, he wasn't going to ridicule her or make her feel guilty. He was her friend. Her first true male friend, which was an interesting and weird thing to acknowledge. She could count on him. Completely.

He made it safe.

She turned to him, still perched on the edge of the hammock, his bare feet swinging. "So, you want to do the Jet Ski thing?"

He raised his head, and this time he was the one doing the kissing, and he meant business. His hand went to the back of her neck to hold her steady, then he used his talented tongue to make her lose her mind.

Finally, he let her go. His head fell to the pillow, hers to his chest. She hadn't stopped petting him, rubbing her hand up and down his swelling erection.

For long minutes, that's all they did. It was quiet and beautiful, and the palm fronds swayed in the breeze.

"Meg?"

"Yes?"

"There's one other thing I've figured out," he said.

She raised her head to see him. "Oh?"

He nodded, but said nothing.

"Well? Are you going to tell me?"

He nodded again. Then his lips curled into that lop-sided grin of his. "It's just that, well, I'm pretty sure I'm in love with you."

18

ALL MEG COULD DO WAS stare. The words reverberated in her head, yet she didn't really understand him. Had Alex just said he loved her?

"Meg?"

He couldn't have meant what she thought he meant. Could he? She'd only gotten here yesterday. She'd been so scared. Of course, she wasn't scared anymore. He was wonderful. But love?

"Meg."

He'd said he thought he was in love with her, which didn't mean that he was *in love* with her, it meant maybe kinda in love. Did he really—

"Meg, if you don't stop squeezing me there, you're not going to be able to play with it later."

She blinked. Looked down. Oh, God, she was squeezing him. Opening her hand quickly, she heard his relieved sigh, which made her look at him again. "Sorry."

"It's okay. I realize I gave you quite a shock."

"Were you kidding?" she asked.

"No."

"Oh."

He smiled at her again. "Is it so impossible that I could love you?"

The tiny hairs on the back of her neck rose as a shiver ran through her body. "Yeah."

His laughter shook the hammock. "Why?"

"Why? We just met."

"Only technically," he said, so calmly she wondered if he understood what he was saying.

"How could you know?" she asked.

"How could I know what I feel, you mean."

She nodded, wanting to believe him.

He raised his head. "Meg, have I upset you?"

"I don't think so," she said.

"Okay."

"But you've sure as hell confused me."

"Why?" he asked.

She thumped him on the arm. "That's my question."

"Fine, I'm cheating. Tell me why this is so bewildering."

She sat up. That wasn't enough. She needed to walk. So she got off the hammock and paced between the two palm trees. "I was just thinking, just a few minutes ago, that you're my first real male friend. And how cool that is. That I could tell you anything and you wouldn't freak out on me."

"Okay…"

"And that I liked you so much," she said.

"Better," he murmured.

"I was thinking that it felt incredible to be with you, and that even if I disappointed you, it would be all right. Because you got it. Got me," she said.

"Uh-huh." He didn't seem quite so calm any more. "But love?"

He'd sat up during her last pass. He put his hands on his knees and studied her. "Remember when I asked you if you'd ever been in love?"

"Uh, yeah. It was yesterday."

"And you said you hadn't."

"No, I said I almost had."

His head tilted to the side as his eyebrow rose.

"Okay, so I said no," she admitted.

"How do you know that love isn't feeling safe? Feeling as though you could tell the one you love anything and he wouldn't freak out on you? What if love is someone who gets you no matter what?" he prodded.

She went to the little table, but her glass hadn't magically refilled itself. "I need to drink now. I'll meet you inside."

He chuckled again, and despite the surreal nature of the conversation, the sound made her insides quiver. Love. *Love?* Nah, it couldn't be that easy. Love had always been a struggle. A thing that was perfect in novels and movies, but not so much in real life. Love wasn't what he described. She wasn't exactly sure what it was, but it wasn't that.

She hurried up the stairs, went right to the phone and ordered two more piña coladas. Then she went to the minibar and debated the wisdom of opening one of the little bottles, but decided on a soda instead. By the time she'd opened it, Alex was there. He stood just inside, his arms crossed casually over his chest.

Meg looked at him, from bare feet to messed-up hair. He had the right combination of features in the right proportions. But that wasn't what made him so handsome.

Those eyes, the way he was looking at her right now. With humor, with patience, with kindness. That crooked grin. So intelligent, but he wasn't the least bit obnoxious about it. Brave. God, so brave. Willing to walk out of the life he knew to uncharted territory, even though the life he had was filled with success and security.

The man thought he loved her. The pull was strong. As tempting as the apple. The setting was certainly perfect for it. She felt strongly about him, so it would be simple to call it love. But…

"It's okay if you don't feel the same way," he finally said.

She sighed. Drank some icy soda. Turned around to face the wall, then turned back. "I don't know."

"That's okay, too."

"Stop being so nice."

He laughed. "Why?"

"Because I'm not that nice. You do know this is first-meeting behavior, right? This isn't what we're really like."

"What are we really like?" he asked, as he crossed to the bed. He sat, pushed some pillows against the headboard and got comfortable.

"I don't know what you're like. But I can be a total bitch. Just catch me when I've had three hours sleep for four days in a row. I cuss like a sailor, I'm selfish beyond belief, and when I'm cranky, everyone for five miles clears out."

"Uh-huh. Like that time when the Porters' cows got sick?"

"Exactly," she said. She walked next to the bed, riled

up now. "That's exactly what I'm talking about. I told a perfectly nice woman to go shove her magazine up her ass. Sweet, huh? I hung up on Terry Okun. Didn't even let her finish her sentence."

He nodded. "As I recall, you told me to go to hell. Straight to hell, and take my goddamn newspaper with me."

"See? I was horrible to you. A total jerk."

"You're right. Of course, that wasn't as bad as when you broke your wrist."

She threw up her hands, spilling soda on the floor. "Okay, okay, that's another perfect example. That's who I really am, Alex. Not this. This isn't close to who I can be."

"Wow, I hadn't thought of that," he said.

"And I'm a chicken, too. I want to leave the mountain. I want to start over, start somewhere new. I want to find out what I like to do. Maybe I like to knit—did you ever think of that?"

"Nope. Never did."

"Well, mister, you don't even know what I'm capable of. I could turn into someone you wouldn't even recognize."

"Right. I'm an idiot for thinking I could know you. At all," he agreed.

"For all *I* know, you could be a bank robber," she said.

He nodded, biting his lower lip. "I might be."

"Or mean to kittens."

"No, I'm pretty nice to kittens, but I'm a son of a bitch when it comes to stupid politicians."

"Yes. Yes, you are. You've said some rotten things,

Alex. You've been mean, and cutting, and just awful. You can't pretend that you haven't, because you've told me yourself."

Alex didn't say a word. He just looked at her. Finally, he let himself smile.

"Oh," she said, as it dawned on her what he'd done.

"I haven't actually seen you when you're sick," he said, his laughter barely contained. "So that would be new."

"Very funny. You're such a smart-ass."

"I'm on my best behavior."

"Double smart-ass. With a side of insufferable jerk," she muttered.

"That's for sure. But I think you knew that already."

"Okay." She sighed, not terribly clear how he'd managed to confuse her more and less at the same time. "We know each other."

He scooted to the end of the bed and patted the place next to him. "Sit."

She did. He took the soda out of her hand and put it on the bedside table. When he turned back to her, he grasped her hands in his.

"I'm thirty-three years old. I've been with a number of women, some of them so terrific it boggled my mind that I didn't love them. I thought I loved Ellen, but when she left me, it wasn't all that bad, so I figured that couldn't be it. During this past year, I've laughed more than I have in the past ten. You've made me think. You've made me feel. You've helped me change my whole life. The only thing missing was being with you in person."

"You love me," she said.

He nodded.

She sighed again, wishing she could just fall. Be as sure and strong as Alex.

"You don't love me back."

"I didn't say that."

"Really."

She wanted to tell him that she loved him. The last thing on earth she wanted to do was hurt him. God knows, he was wonderful, and she cared, deeply. "I just don't know. I'm sorry."

"That's okay. We have three more days," he said.

She had to grin at that. "Three days should do it, then?"

"I'm thinking two, but three at the most."

"Ah."

"That's another bad thing about me," he said. "I get all cocky at the least provocation. Just so you know."

God, what his smile did to her insides. "Yeah, I got that."

"Drinks coming?"

"Any minute," she said.

"Great. I'm gonna go wait outside." He looked her over once, briefly. "If you wanted to get naked, that would be nice."

"Nice."

He kissed her. Then kissed her again, harder. By the time he pulled back, she was very agreeable about the proposition.

He left her sitting on the bed. With too many thoughts in her head, and a puzzled ache in her heart.

ALEX STOOD AT THE END of the path, waiting for the golf cart. Yeah, Charlie could come by, but Alex didn't care.

Meg needed some space, and that's what mattered. What surprised him the most was that he felt calm.

It was good that he'd told her. Good that he'd admitted it to himself. It would have been better if she'd felt the same way, but he was pretty sure she'd come to see that what they had was the real thing.

What he wanted was for her to leave the mountain. To get away from her past and start living her future. With him.

Which probably wasn't what he was going to get.

He'd take what she offered. No question there. And in time, perhaps, she'd see that she didn't owe her very life to her work.

It was a fine line to walk. He had a real tendency to think his conclusions were brilliant and that anyone who didn't heed his advice was a fool. It came with the territory, he supposed. He couldn't think of one person in his professional life who didn't have that attitude, but when it came to real relationships with people who mattered, being all-knowing definitely put a crimp in the flow of ideas.

Meg had a right to choose, all by herself. He didn't live her life and he didn't face her demons. But he'd sure like her to be there when he faced his.

Leaving the paper wasn't going to be easy. Since he'd made the decision, he'd come up with a dozen reasons why the whole notion was patently ridiculous. But in the end, the pain of staying was worse than the pain of trying something new.

Meg's pain just wasn't bad enough. If it were, she'd make a change. It was not his place to force the issue.

What he could do was make love to her.

Speaking of which, there was the golf cart, and the drinks, and God, he hoped Meg was naked.

Enough. Now was the time to act. Ask not what Meg could do for him, but what he could do for Meg. That it made him happier than any human had a right to feel was beside the point.

MEG HEARD ALEX COMING UP the steps, and thought about posing provocatively. Only, every pose she thought of seemed amazingly cheesy. So she just dropped her head on her arm, and her other hand casually on her hip, so that it kind of covered how she pooched at the stomach. The naked part would distract him, anyway. Whatever else he was, he was a guy. Bless his heart.

Oh, the smile when he walked into the room. What could possibly beat that? It made everything tingly, which was a hell of a lot for a smile to accomplish.

He brought her a drink, which meant she had to uncover the pooch, but it was a really good drink. She sipped and watched him strip off his clothes.

That didn't take long—it was just swim trunks. Once again, he was very happy to see her. It would be so hard to be a man, she thought. So much pressure.

Before he got into bed with her, he took a long sip. Then he put his glass down and lay down next to her, facing her.

"You make me very happy," he said, his voice soft and low, with a hint of a quiver just behind the words.

"Yeah?"

He nodded. "No matter what."

"So, even if I can't quit and run off to a cabin in Colorado, we can still be friends?"

"I'd like that," he told her.

"Me, too."

"Sometimes friends get together from time to time. They go places like, I don't know, a tropical island," he said.

"Really?" she asked, much more comfortable with this train of thought.

"Uh-huh." He scooted a little closer and slipped his leg between hers.

She took the hint and curled up next to him, putting his arm around her waist, her head in the crook of his shoulder. "How often do these hypothetical friends do this kind of thing?"

"I don't know. Once a quarter has a nice ring to it. Hypothetically."

"Good to know. Now how about a not-so-hypothetical kiss?"

He touched her cheek with the back of his hand, as if he were touching something breakable. Something precious.

His kiss was even better. It was crazy, but it felt different. He'd kissed her all kinds of ways since she'd gotten here. With passion, with tenderness, with animal heat and childlike happiness. But this was something else. It was as if he was giving himself with his lips, with his tongue. And asking for her in return.

There was no way to say no.

She put her hand on his cheek and she kissed him

back. With nothing in the way, no shields, no hiding. This was everything she was—the good, the bad, the fear, the courage. Take her. Have her.

He moaned, his voice warming all the cold places deep inside. A joining in a way she'd never been joined.

With fluttering eyelids and her heart beating a new rhythm, she burrowed closer, wanting to touch him everywhere, to be touched.

His hand moved down her side, then to her back as he pulled her tight. She felt his erection and the power he had even before he was inside her.

She shifted, wanting him. Now, *now*.

He spread himself on top of her with his full weight, heavy, but good, too. Then he braced his arms on either side of her, lifting just enough.

His knees parted her thighs. She raised her legs and wrapped them around his hips, wanting to open herself as completely as she could.

For a long moment, he didn't move. His eyes were open, and they were focused on nothing but hers. She felt everything. Her heart, the muscles holding her legs up, every breath, the wetness between her legs. It was all in high definition.

"No matter what," he whispered. "You're the best thing that's happened to me that I can remember. When you're cranky, when you're silly, when you're sexy, when you're sleeping. All of it. All of you."

She nodded, wanting so badly to believe him. Tears came and spilled, trickling down her temples, hotter than her skin.

Alex dipped his head and licked the trail just over her

cheek. An impossibly intimate act. He brought the tears back to her, let her taste them on his tongue.

It was then that he entered her. Slowly this time, a hundred light years from what had happened in the shower. It ached, how carefully he pushed in. Not because she was afraid, but because it was the sweetest of agonies.

His mouth widened and narrowed, his tongue delved inside, then swept her teeth, only to find something new to touch, to share.

She breathed his breath.

Still, he wasn't in her completely. He trembled above her, where their bodies touched. She wasn't even sure whether it was his trembling she felt, or her own.

Finally, he was there. Buried inside her. Another connection. Deep, pure. He pulled back again so he could meet her gaze. And as he moved, as he loved her, she knew what it was to be seen completely. To be whole in another's eyes. In his heart.

She closed her eyes, unable to bear it. Turned her head. Lifted her hips, forced him to move, to go back to the sex, to what she could understand.

He kissed her temple where the tears had dried, and he made sure she came. That they both came.

When it was over, he rolled to her side. Not quite touching. Just being close.

She didn't cry again, but she wanted to.

19

ALEX STARED AT THE CEILING as he tried to figure out what the hell had just happened. He'd never felt more connected to another human being, and then she was gone, as if a door had slammed shut.

A gentleman would have stopped, asked her what was wrong. Alex had just been too far gone. Granted, she hadn't stopped moving. She'd thrust her hips, raked his back with her hands. If he hadn't known her so well, he probably wouldn't have noticed the abrupt change. What had surprised him almost as much as whatever had made her turn from him was how she'd come. She'd screamed, clenched her muscles so hard she'd triggered his own wickedly fierce orgasm.

Now she lay next to him, so warm her heat radiated to his body. He turned to find her chest rising and falling fast, like that of a long-distance runner. Every part of her was tense. She stared up at the same ceiling, her lips slightly parted, her skin still moist with sweat.

What had he done wrong? What had he said? Just as he was about to ask her, she startled him by sitting up, swinging her feet to the floor. She picked up her piña colada, and for the next few minutes, all she did was drink. Big gulps through the straw.

He watched her, wishing her hair wasn't covering so much of her back. He couldn't get a bead on what was going through her mind, and it was killing him to think he'd upset her.

The hell with it. He sat up. "Meg?"

"Yeah?"

"You want to talk about it?" he asked.

"Nope."

"Okay."

She sighed, still not facing him. "I'm sorry, I didn't mean to be so bitchy. Of course I want to talk, and I will, as soon as I figure out what's going on."

"Fair enough. Tell you what. You just stay put." He got out of bed and headed for the bathroom. Once there, he ran some warm water, got himself cleaned up and fixed her a warm washcloth. After snagging a towel, he went back to the bedroom. She was right where he'd left her, looking beautiful, if a little sad. He didn't think it was because she'd finished her drink. She needed some time, that's all. And if she decided that she wanted only friendship from him, well, then, he'd come to terms.

"Thank you," she said.

He nodded. "I'm going to put on some clothes," he said. "You take your time, okay? Whenever you're ready to go out, just let me know."

His gaze moved to the alarm clock next to the empty glass. Eleven o'clock. They'd been together for twenty-three hours. It felt like weeks. More, it felt like a year.

"I'm sorry, Alex," she said.

"Don't be. Just relax and smell the ocean."

That got a smile out of her. It seemed like a good time

to make his exit. He went for the stairs. She stopped him with a hand on his arm.

He waited. She didn't say anything, but the way she looked at him made him want to comfort her.

"I just need to get my head together," she said.

"I'd imagine so."

"You get to be cranky about this, if you want."

He leaned over and kissed her forehead. "No need. Just remember there's nothing you have to do."

She nodded.

Alex couldn't help it, his gaze moved down her lovely body, fascinated by her beauty. It was the first time he'd paid attention when she was naked like this, when he wasn't consumed with need for her body. Not that he didn't need her, but it was a banked sensation, wrapped in gauze for the time being.

She really was stunning, but that was only an added bonus. He would have felt this way if she'd looked different. He hadn't needed those dark eyes gazing at him when he was in D.C.

He stopped. Just stopped. She would let him know when she was ready to talk. Instead, he'd walk up the stairs and wait. He would read, listen to music. And think.

DESPITE ALEX'S kind gesture, Meg went to the bathroom and got cleaned up there. It took a while to untangle her hair, but once that was done, she went to the closet and pulled out a pair of khaki shorts and a T-shirt. She smiled as she pulled on yet another pair of white panties, and her thoughts moved straight to the man upstairs.

Could he truly be in love with her? He'd sounded so

sincere. He'd looked at her with naked eyes, a voice raw with emotion.

She had to stop thinking of him as Alex, and remember that he was also DCWatcher. The one person in her life she had no reason to mistrust. She'd told him so much about herself and she hadn't censored much. Did he remember that stuff? Or was he so taken with the atmosphere that all he could see was what he wanted to see?

The sound of a golf cart approaching the bungalow chased her thoughts to the background. She crossed the room quickly and looked out the window. "Alex."

"Yes?" he called down.

"We've got trouble."

She heard his bare feet on the stairs, and then he was standing next to her, both of them watching Charlie Hanover, looking hot and irritable as he pulled off the path right up to the side of the building. "Oh, no."

"It's all right." Alex squeezed her shoulder. "I'll be back."

He turned to leave, but before he took even a few steps, Meg heard Tina's voice from just outside their door.

"Hello, again."

She watched Charlie's eyes widen in horror as two pairs of feet hurried down the wooden stairs outside. Tina and Walter came into view, flanking Charlie's cart.

"Oh, no. You're not doing this again," Charlie said.

"Doing what again?" Tina asked, the picture of innocence.

"I know you're hiding him. I just want to talk to him, that's all. If you've got a problem with that, call the editor of the *New York Times*, lady. There's such a thing as freedom of the press."

Meg turned to Alex, but he wasn't there. He'd crossed the room and was opening the door. "What are you doing?" she whispered.

"It's enough. I'll get rid of him. I won't be five minutes." Then he was gone.

She wasn't about to sit here and let him face this alone. She dashed for the door, and by the time she was on the stairs, Alex was standing in front of Charlie's cart, but Alex was looking at Tina.

"Thank you," he said. "Both of you. But I've got it covered."

"We could call Mr. Castellano," Walter said.

"No need. It's fine."

Tina moved a little closer to Hanover. "The man is on vacation. You should be ashamed of yourself."

Charlie didn't give her so much as a glance. "So what the hell's going on, Alex? You've caused quite a stir."

"I imagine so."

As quietly as she could, Meg joined Tina as the older woman headed back to her own bungalow.

"Should we stay?" Tina whispered.

Meg took her hand and gave it a gentle squeeze. "No, it's okay. Thank you."

Tina nodded and kept on going. Meg stayed where she was, never taking her eyes off of Alex.

Charlie climbed out of the cart. He looked like he'd been in his own island hell. His shirt was wrinkled and sweaty, his hair, what there was of it, stuck up at odd angles. He was sunburned and his lips looked parched.

"You broke the code, buddy," he said. "Didn't anybody tell you that's not the way things are done?"

"I was tired of the way things are done," Alex said. In contrast, he looked cool and calm. His hands were in the pockets of his jeans, and his Hawaiian shirt billowed with the breeze.

"What the hell did you think you'd accomplish?" Charlie walked closer to Alex, who didn't budge an inch. "Did you think you'd end up the hero in all this?"

"I wasn't aiming for hero, no."

"You've seriously pissed off every newsperson in Washington, did you know that? Not to mention the entire Senate and House. No one's going to talk to you. You don't have a single source left in the city."

"Okay."

"Okay?" Charlie's eyes narrowed as if he were studying an unknown species. "You destroyed Senator Bradley. You told the world he's been manipulating the appropriations committee to get his brother-in-law's company a sweetheart deal from the Navy. You've accused Gary Shayner of taking bribes from the gaming commission."

"I know."

"The only thing I can think of is that you're dying. Are you?"

Alex chuckled. "No, Charlie. Sorry to disappoint you, but I'm not dying. In fact, I'm just starting to live."

"Oh, Christ," Charlie said, loudly. "Don't tell me you've found religion."

"The only thing I've found is my integrity," Alex said, not rising to the bait. If anything, he lowered his voice. "But then, I don't expect you to understand that."

"Cut the sanctimonious crap. I've known you for too many years."

"And I've known you. Charlie, go home. I'm not going to do this. I'm on vacation. When I get back to D.C., you can lay into me, but not now. Not here."

"You think after all the crap you've put me through I'm gonna sit on the sidelines? You're no better than the rest of us. I've seen you in action. You wouldn't know integrity if it bit you in the ass."

Alex shrugged. "What you believe is immaterial. I'm taking myself out of the game. That's all. I'm no longer willing to abuse the system. I'm out. I'm gone. It's over."

"Unless you're planning on living in a cave somewhere, I don't think it's going to be quite so neat. People are going to want proof."

Alex looked out at the ocean for a moment. "Shit, Charlie. I've got proof. You've got proof. Everyone tapes everything, we write down everything, we never let a bad deed go unrecorded. I've just decided it's about time I shared what I know."

"Oh, my God. You are amazing. Just amazing." He stepped closer to Alex, and Meg could see he was trembling. His face was red, and she didn't think it was sunburn.

"And you know what? I'm gonna crucify you, Rosten. I'm gonna spill every tiny tidbit I've collected over the years. By the time I'm through with you, you won't get a job writing for the *Pennysaver*. You got that?"

"Whatever makes you happy," Alex said.

Charlie stared at him for a long time, his body still

vibrating. Finally, his gaze shifted to Meg. "Is she the reason?"

"In a way."

"What does that mean?"

Alex turned to look at her. His smile was sweet and easy, not the least bit strained. "Because I want to be a good man for her. She deserves that."

Ignoring Alex, Charlie started toward her. "What's your name, honey?"

Alex stopped him with a firm grip on his arm. "Get out, Charlie. Now. You're not getting anything more from me, or her, so you might as well pack it in."

"She can speak for herself, can't she?" He shook his arm loose, but he didn't move toward her. "He's just as dirty as the rest of us, sweetheart. Once the novelty wears off, he'll be begging to come back."

"I don't think so," Meg said. Her shoulders went back and her gaze zeroed in on his. "You have no idea who you're messing with."

Alex walked between Charlie and Meg. His body had tensed, although she could see he was still in control. "Get out of here, Charlie. Write whatever the hell you want to, I don't care." He walked to Meg, capturing her hand as he went to the stairs.

"I'm not letting this go, Rosten. I'm gonna find out everything. You're through. You hear me?"

Alex walked her up the stairs, opened the door and followed Meg inside. He closed and locked the door behind them. "Sorry about that."

"Can he cause trouble for you?"

Alex shook his head."

"He sounded serious."

"He sounded desperate. There's a difference. He just can't stand it that he couldn't ruin me personally. He hates that I blew the whistle on myself."

"I think I understand what it is you did. And what kind of courage it took," Meg said.

"Not really."

"Quit being so damn humble and let me say this. I'm amazingly proud of you. And somewhat intimidated."

He laughed. "By me? Are you kidding? Don't you get it? All this has come about because of you. Not just because I want to make you proud, but because I want to be like you."

"What? Like me? Why?"

"Because you tell the truth whether it's pleasant or not. You don't pull any punches. You never let me get away with any crap. You're a tiger when you need to be. I admire the hell out of you," he said.

All she could do was stare at him. That wasn't at all how she saw herself, and it was a little frightening. But it was also kind of exciting.

Was the excitement about Alex, about the idea of true love, romance, all those wonderful things he represented, or was the excitement about finding out who she was? Who she was meant to be?

"I love my work," she said. "I'll never stop wanting to be a vet."

"I know."

"But that doesn't mean I have to be a vet on the mountain. I could work in a hospital, or a clinic. I could work anywhere."

Alex smiled. Just smiled.

"I want to travel, too. I've always wanted to go to Australia. And India," she said.

"Yeah?"

Her heart pounded in her chest as she looked into his dark, wonderful eyes. "Did you take dancing lessons?"

"Huh?"

"When we were in the disco. You danced really well. How come?" she asked.

"Yes, I took lessons. Remember when swing was so popular? 'Big Bad Voodoo Daddy' and all that?"

"Did you go alone?"

He nodded. He still hadn't lost his somewhat bemused grin.

"I did. But it wasn't simply to find my inner Fred Astaire. I was trying to pick up chicks."

She swatted him on the arm. "But you had fun, huh?"

"A lot. Although I rarely get to use my dazzling skills," he confessed.

"What else have you done?"

He laughed, looked up to the loft, then back at her. "That seems like a pretty broad question. Can you narrow it down just a smidge?"

"Classes. Courses. Languages on tape. What have you done?" She knew she was talking wildly, flinging her hands about, but dammit, this was important.

"You know, we've talked about this stuff before. Remember? In the wee hours?"

"I need more, okay?"

"You got it," he said, sounding very serious. He

crossed his arms over his chest. "I've taken refresher courses in French and German."

"Cool."

"I took a cooking class once. Thai food," he added.

"Do you cook?"

"Rarely. But I don't hate it. I just don't seem to have a lot of time for it. You should see my collection of take-out menus. Extensive."

"Where have you been? Traveled?" she asked, leading him to the bed. She sat down on the edge and he joined her, never once breaking their eye contact.

"Let's see. I've been to a lot of Europe. All work related. Hawaii. South Africa, also work related."

"And just for pleasure?"

"I went to Camp Winnatonka when I was eleven."

"Good experience?"

"I got a rash. Poison ivy. I also kissed Lisa Jackson, but then she told on me and I had to wash pots in the commissary."

Meg grinned. "Was it worth it?"

"It didn't become worth it for a couple more years," he confessed.

"When did you first do it?"

"Do it?" Alex asked, wide eyed. "Wait, is *this* Camp Winnatonka?"

"Don't make me pinch you."

"When I was sixteen. She was eighteen. It was in a very small car at a disreputable carnival. I was worried for a long time that my dick would fall off from some horrible disease. Now, may I ask a question?"

She shook her head. "Not yet. First let me finish."

"Fair enough," he said.

"What do you want to do?"

"When?"

"After you leave Washington. Aside from writing, what do you want to do? In Colorado, or wherever you end up," she added.

"Ah. I haven't spent too much time thinking about that because I was so busy with the career suicide and all, but I do like fishing. Trout fishing. And kayaking. I'd like to do more of that," he said.

"What else?" she asked, scooting closer to him. She felt as if her heart would beat out of her chest.

"Uh, well, now that you mention it, dancing would be good. Take time to listen to my records. Write letters to people. Not e-mail. Letters on stationery with my initials embossed. I'd like to read fiction." His voice quickened and she knew he was getting it. Feeling this connection that was beyond electric. "You know how hard it is for me to find time to read fiction? Damn, I want a library. A whole room, like something out of Sherlock Holmes, complete with a roaring fireplace, wing chairs and one of those ladders so I can reach the hardbacks on the top shelf."

Meg closed her eyes for a minute, letting it all sink in. He liked to kayak. She did, too. A lot. And whitewater rafting, which she'd only done once, but it was a major rush.

"My turn yet?" he asked.

"One more. What are you like in the morning?"

"Before coffee?"

She nodded.

"Not pretty. But you wouldn't have to run for cover."

"After coffee?" she asked.

"Much better."

She smiled. Swallowed as the pieces came together like the most perfect puzzle, creating a new picture she'd never even dreamed before.

"Now?" he said.

She nodded.

"What the hell's going on?"

Laughter bubbled up, and it took her a minute to chill. "I figured out I'm scared to death."

"Of?"

"Every damn thing you can think of. Quitting. Leaving the mountain. Loving someone. Loving you."

He nodded, staring at her as if it would help. "And?"

"I just watched one of the most courageous things I've ever seen. The way you talked to Charlie. But that isn't even the important part. You did this all so quietly. I'm a little pissed that you didn't tell me, but I'm also awed that you made this huge, life-changing decision on your own. With no fanfare, no whining. And then you just did it. You don't know the outcome, you're not hedging your bets. You just walked right into your new life. Dammit, you are a hero. And here I am, terrified to leave the mountain I was born on. Terrified. But all of a sudden I'm excited, too. You know, I've never been overseas. Never. I love the water and I love to read, but I'm so tired, I can't get past page ten of anything before I fall asleep. And yes, I know you know that, but it doesn't matter, because you're here now, and you're real now, and I need to say it out loud. I don't want to end up on that mountain for the rest of my life. I just don't."

"What would you like to do?"

God, the way he looked at her. As if he could barely contain himself. "I want to have options. I want to think things through so I don't run off half-cocked. And then I want to try things that scare the bejesus out of me."

"Wow."

"And I'd really like to explore the whole notion of doing this with you."

His smile came slowly, but it was worth it. "You would?"

"Yeah."

"Cool."

She put her hands on her hips. "Cool? That's it?"

"Not even close. But if I show you how happy I am right now, we probably won't be able to continue the discussion."

"We have three more days to talk," she said.

"Why, Dr. Becker. Are you suggesting we do something carnal?"

"If you're up for it."

He chuckled. "Considering all we've been through in the last twenty-four hours, I'm damn proud it didn't fall off. In other words, not yet."

"It's okay. I don't care."

"You mean, you don't love me for my sexual prowess?" he teased.

"I don't hate you for it."

He shook his head. "I'm not sure if I should be pleased or insulted."

She wrapped her arms around his neck and they both

fell back on the bed. He felt so good against her. "Pleased. Trust me."

"I can't deny you anything. But you already knew that."

"Yeah. I did. Which, by the way, I won't hold you to, but I love the sentiment."

"Good."

"But that's not the important part, either."

He ran his hand down her arm, then pulled her closer. "What's the important part?"

"I'm pretty sure I'm in love with you," Meg confessed.

He inhaled a little faster, his hands gripped her a bit tighter, but other than that, he held it together well. "Pretty sure?"

She nodded. "You still have all that mess back in Washington. I still have to figure out how I'm going to leave the mountain. There are money issues, and where to go, and—oh, crap, I just assumed you wanted to do all that with me, and if you don't that's okay, because—"

He put two fingers on her lips. "Yes. I want to do all that with you."

"Really?"

"Yeah."

"It's not going to be easy," she murmured.

"Nothing worthwhile ever is."

She put her head on his shoulder. "I eat Oreos in bed."

"Do you share?" he joked.

"With you? Something could be arranged."

"I talk to myself when I write," he admitted.

"Are you funny?"

"I have no idea. But I seriously doubt it. Usually, a great many curse words are involved."

"I can handle that."

"So I take it you're pleased?" he asked. "About coming here?"

She looked up into his eyes. "Best gift ever."

He kissed her then. A sweet, deep, loving kiss that gave her goose bumps. That gave her strength.

"We're gonna be great together," he whispered.

She believed him.

Epilogue

One year later...

[DCWatcher] First, don't be mad, Meg.

[MtnVet] Don't be mad? What's going on, Alex?

[DCWatcher] Just...don't be mad. And go to the door.

[MtnVet] What door?

[DCWatcher] The front door.

[MtnVet] K. Be right back.

[MtnVet] Alex?

[DCWatcher] Took you long enough.

[MtnVet] What have you done? And the flowers are gorgeous, thank you.

[DCWatcher] You're welcome. Open the envelope.

[MtnVet] Alex!!!!

[DCWatcher] Yes?

[MtnVet] Escapades?

[DCWatcher] It was pretty good last time, wasn't it?

[MtnVet] Best vacation ever, but how can you?

[DCWatcher] I have my ways.

[MtnVet] What's your editor going to say? The book is due next week.

[DCWatcher] It'll be done.

[MtnVet] So you took solitaire off your laptop?

[DCWatcher] Ha! You're so funny.

[MtnVet] Not to mention my work.

[DCWatcher] You can take some time off.

[MtnVet] I've only been working there four months. What are they going to think?

[DCWatcher] Who cares? They love you. They want you. They need you. Oh, wait. Maybe that's me.

[MtnVet] Well, that's not playing fair.

[DCWatcher] It's just the facts, ma'am.

[MtnVet] Five days, four nights. The same bungalow.

[DCWatcher] So???

[MtnVet] I can't say no to you.

[DCWatcher] Then my plan worked.

[MtnVet] Maybe I can...

[DCWatcher] No, you can't. Besides, the reservation is in, the plane tickets purchased, so you must say yes.

[MtnVet] Of course I'm going to say yes.

[DCWatcher] Excellent. Now, one last instruction.

[MtnVet] I'm not taking off any clothes.

[DCWatcher] No, I want you to turn around.

[MtnVet] ???

[DCWatcher] Just do it!

Meg turned slowly, not sure what to expect. She was in their kitchen, having her coffee before she had to go to the clinic. She knew Alex was at the library, where he was doing some research on the book. So what could he have done now?

"You sneaky bastard."

Alex stood at the kitchen door, his laptop still in his hand. His grin warmed her all the way to her toes. "Surprise."

"You're supposed to be working," she accused.

"I took a break," he said.

"So I see."

He put the computer on the counter as she stood up. They met in the middle. He pulled her close and kissed her, as always, curling her toes.

"Yes," she whispered, when she could speak again.

"I thought you might say that. And I'm hoping you'll say it again, when I tell you I've made arrangements for us to get married, right there on the island."

She laughed and at the very same time her eyes filled with tears. "Oh, my God. Alex."

"Is that a yes?"

She kissed him on the lips, on the cheeks, all over his face. "Yes, that's a yes. A hundred times yes."

He laughed, too. "That's good, because I already sent in the deposit."

"So we're really gonna go the whole nine yards, huh?"

He nodded. "So far, so good."

It hadn't been easy for either of them, but they'd

come so far in the last year. They'd both left their old lives behind and started out fresh and new. His writing was going well, and she loved her new job at the Boulder animal hospital. Living together had been an incredible joy from day one, but getting married? It was the icing on a very incredible cake.

Alex bent his head and nibbled on the sensitive skin of her neck. "Are you sure that you don't want to take off any of those clothes?"

There was only one thing she could do. She pinched him. Right on his sexy butt. And then she walked him out of the kitchen, straight up to the bedroom.

* * * * *

*Look for more
sun, sex and sand
in February 2006!
Pick up the next
exciting book in the
24 HOURS ISLAND FLING
miniseries—
TALL, TANNED & TEXAN
by Kimberly Raye.*

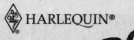
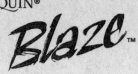